Vikings at Dino's

Also by

William H. Duquette

Travels with Michael:

Very Truly Run After

A Little High Tension (forthcoming)

The Known World:

Through Darkest Zymurgia

Vikings at Dino's

A Novel of Lunch and Mayhem

by
William H. Duquette

Zymurgia House, 2016

Glendale, California
ZymurgiaHouse.com

Printed in the United States of America

Second Printing, 2017

ISBN: 978-0692716724

Cover illustration:
Jason Bach, jasonbachcartoons.com

Cover design:
Julie Davis, General Glyphics, Dallas Texas

To Jane and the kids

Time is an illusion;

lunchtime doubly so.

— *Douglas Adams*

Chapter 1

When the Viking war party burst through the front entrance of Dino's Burgers & More, it was second nature for me to slide quietly under my table. When you're small for your age, it's often useful not to be noticed. Once on the floor I waited on events, peering out as best I could past the swivel seats, and wondering what was going to happen. Vikings are not a usual sight at Dino's. I could tell they were Vikings, because they were wearing bear-skins and helmets with horns on them. There were six or seven of them, all heavily armed. I use the word "heavily" with precision—the battle axes they were toting so nonchalantly looked too big for me to lift. I admit to being suspicious of their motives. Most people I see walking into Dino's, I figure they are there to eat something. Vikings, well, you have to assume Vikings are there for plunder. The big question in my mind was, were they planning to plunder the living or the dead?

The axe blow taken by the man near the door resolved all of my doubts, so the second blow (which bisected one of Dino's burgers, the fellow eating it, and the green Formica top of the table he was sitting at) was completely uncalled for. I had seen enough; it was time for Plan A. While the Viking in question was trying to free his axe, I was slithering across the brown tile floor, flat on my stomach, heedless of stray french fries and dropped packets of ketchup. By the time he had yanked it loose from the table top I had slid under a beige plastic bench seat and slipped

10

out the door, nipping neatly behind the last Viking to enter. Once outside I put a dusty minivan between me and the restaurant, and squatted down by its rear bumper to catch my breath. This was a necessary step—it turns out that Vikings don't smell so good. Then I took a quick look around from my spot on the pavement.

There were the usual cars, including a cherry-looking Model A I'd not seen before, but the only jarring note was the dragon-headed longship parked—or, I guess, moored—between me and the fence where I'd locked my bike. I looked it over as best I could from where I crouched. It looked like a longship from a Hollywood movie, except that there weren't any shields hanging along the sides. It also looked deserted, which was more to the point. The number one question in my mind was the size of the raiding party. Were the Vikings in the restaurant all there were, or had they left one of their number behind to stand guard on the ship? Was I likely to be bisected as I mounted my bicycle? I rose to my feet so that I could see the restaurant through the windows of the minivan. I couldn't see much through the tinted glass, even after I wiped the dust off with the sleeve of my hoodie, but the Vikings all seemed to be busy inside. Since I couldn't stay where I was, and the bike was my fastest ticket elsewhere, I decided to chance it.

I glided around the outside of the lot, keeping as low as I could (not hard) while hopping over the concrete blocks at the head of each parking space. I was careful to keep as many cars as possible between me and the building. Still no sign of any guards on the longship. That surprised me a little, until I realized that a casual thief would need to go rent a flatbed truck and a crane before they could haul it away. The Vikings had nothing to worry about, though I did wonder how they had managed to moor the ship there in the first place.

The longship was sitting across the whole row of parking spaces by the fence, its mast standing tall and vertical and its hull level, though there were no chocks or braces holding it that way. It was just lying there on its keel, perfectly balanced, waiting for its bloodthirsty crew to come back and sail it away. It occurred to me that it was lucky for the Vikings that they hadn't come during the breakfast rush, or those spots would have been filled with contractor's trucks and police cars. They'd have had to go plunder somewhere else.

There was just enough room between the side of the longship and the fence for me to scoot through to where my bike was chained up, and I did that. I'd have liked to take a peek over the rail, just in passing, but it was well over my head. I patted the hull as I went by, though. It was made of overlapping planks of unweathered wood, and it was perfectly dry. Shouldn't it have gotten wet on the trip here? Then I felt foolish. Whatever means, magical or otherwise, the Vikings had used to get here, they certainly hadn't come by water. And why shouldn't living Vikings have a newish longship?

And why should there be living Vikings hacking and slaying at Dino's? I filed that. When you're executing Plan A, you have to stay focussed.

I reached my bike without incident, and thirty seconds later, lock and chain heavy in the pocket of my hoodie, I was pedaling out the driveway and down the street. My strong inclination was to put as much distance as possible between me and the sort of folks who kill first and plunder afterwards. My bike's your basic beach cruiser, and usually it's all I need, but that day I wished I had a serious road bike so that I could shift all the way up to the top gear and get out of there even faster.

It was the natural reaction, but I soon thought better of it. When you're small for your age you like to keep track of your enemies, so as not to run into them unexpectedly. I didn't know where the Vikings had come from, or where they were going, but I wanted to know the direction they took when they left. Besides, I'm nosy. When they moved that longship, I wanted to see how they did it.

So I pedaled around the corner and down the alley, pulling up behind Motor World Auto Parts. It's more or less across the street from Dino's, and I'd long ago noticed that the store had a metal utility ladder bolted to its back wall, the kind where the first four or five rungs are in a sort of locked cabinet so that small people bent on escaping from random hooligans won't be able to do so. The owner might as well have not locked it, though, given that he'd parked a trash bin in front of it. I used my bike as a stepladder up to the top of the bin, and in a few more moments I was on the roof and peeking at Dino's through the letter "A" in the store's sign.

I was just in time. The Vikings were swaggering out of the burger joint; apparently the raid had been a roaring success. One was laden with coats and jackets, while another had a dirty canvas bag of what appeared to be shoes and boots. A third carried a dozen or so plastic trays, the kind they bring you your food on. Several were munching french fries out of white paper bags, and the one at the end of the line—a guy with an enormous red mustache—was eating what looked like a cheeseburger and carrying a small, heavy sack. Jewelry? Coins from the cash register? I wondered whether the burger was the one I'd abandoned, and if so I hoped he would choke on it. I couldn't make out what they were saying, but I could hear them laughing and joking back and forth. Cutting people in half and stealing their french fries, it's all in a day's work.

As they were vaulting one by one into the longship—no trouble for them, stupid giants—I noticed a flickering glow coming from the front windows of Dino's, and a roaring noise. There was a boom, and a burst of flame shot out the drive-up window, and a moment later all of the other windows blew out in a shower of safety glass. The smell of burgers and fries billowed across the street, along with vast, greasy clouds of smoke. There were no screams.

I heard a Viking shout, and turned back to the longship. I saw the sail go up, and then the ship vanished into the smoke. Or perhaps it just vanished. It was gone, anyway, silently and easily.

So much for knowing where the Vikings were headed. I called 911 on my phone, trying to make my voice deeper, and then watched Dino's Burgers and More burn. Had Dino been in today? I hoped not. I'd never actually spoken to him, but he had a cheerful attitude, and I liked him. When I heard the approaching sirens, I climbed back down to my bike and pedaled home.

I stuck close by my computer all that evening, tracking the local news on the 'net and pondering. When you're small for your age, you learn to take time to think; it's the only way to keep one step ahead of the other guy. Since you have to take two steps to his one, that's important. Anyway, KCE News Radio reported on the fire, but there was no mention of Vikings or longships or battle axes. It was simply reported as one of those tragic things that happens sometimes. Apparently I was the only (surviving) eye-witness, and of course I hadn't stuck around to be interviewed.

I didn't know what to make of the whole affair. It was unprecedented. Viking raiders had never invaded Dino's Burgers before, nor any of the other fast food joints in town. It had never even occurred to me as a possibility. And though I'd never been much for studying history, I knew perfectly well that Vikings were not a 21st-Century phenomenon.

So what to do? I recoiled at the thought of calling the police. I could just hear the conversation in my head:

Me: Hi, I'd like to report some Viking raiders.

Officer on duty: <click>

I mean, really. Bloodthirsty Vikings looting and pillaging and killing in Corey's End? Who'd believe me? And anyway, I don't like talking with cops.

When I went to bed, I was sure of only two things: first, that wherever they came from the Vikings weren't supposed to be in my town, and second, that it was going to be a long time, if ever, before I ate another cheeseburger at Dino's Burgers & More. I'd have to find a new place for lunch.

That was Monday. On Tuesday they hit Chicken-to-Go, a take-out a couple of blocks from what was left of Dino's. It's a tiny little place, the kind of chicken place where the smell can make you hungry from a block away. I don't go there often, because there's no place to sit down. I either have to sit on the curb, or else take my lunch all the way over to Corey Park where there are picnic benches, but by the time I get there it gets cold. The chicken's OK, though, not great, but OK, and the prices are good.

Most people use the drive-through at Chicken-To-Go, and I was the only customer in the place. I had just paid the man, a new guy I hadn't seen before, and was turning to go when I noticed the longship parked by the curb. It now had a row of too-familiar plastic trays hanging all along the side, like shields, and it presented me with a problem. I couldn't use Plan A, because the only door would lead into the arms of the Vikings. Time for Plan B. I couldn't duck under a table, since there weren't any, so I hurled myself into a corner behind the cabinet that holds the trash bin, and made myself as small as I could. That's pretty small. Then I covered my face with the hood of my hoodie. Don't want to be seen? Cover your face. People see faces even when they aren't looking for them.

I tried not to listen as the Vikings took all of the change from the register, three buckets of chicken (a phone order waiting for pick-up), a wad of napkins, and the life of the new guy at the counter. I dared a peek at them as they were going out the door. It was the same group I had seen at Dino's (as if there were any doubt), although several of them had discarded their bear skins for nylon jackets I was pretty sure I recognized. Fortunately for me, they didn't torch the place like they had Dino's.

When next I looked the longship had vanished, and I got out of there fast. I'd grabbed my bag of chicken as I dove for cover, so at least I wasn't going to go hungry. I didn't bother calling 911 this time, because there didn't seem to be any point. There was no fire, and the counter guy was pretty thoroughly dead. The Talking Head on the KCE News that night called it a robbery and said there were no suspects. I could have given him an earful, but I didn't. Vikings! Hah!

Wednesday it was Rickenbacker's Pizza. I don't usually eat at

Rickenbacker's; the pizza's good, but it's kind of expensive, and even the individual size is way too much for me. On the other hand, it's quiet, and it's usually not too busy, so long as I have lunch a little later than usual. The atmosphere is nice, lots of dark wood and fake Tiffany lamps and pictures of World War I fighter planes. More importantly, Rickenbacker's has tables, big solid tables with red-and-white-checked oilskin table cloths, and when the Vikings showed up I made good use of the one I'd been sitting at in the corner over by the video games. I peeked out after the thudding and chopping noises had subsided, and saw them walking out the front door with five pizza boxes, a couple of pitchers of beer they hadn't paid for, and what looked to be the restaurant's entire supply of pizza pans. I didn't wait to see if burning the place was on their agenda; I was out the back door the moment the front door swung shut. After my close call at Chicken-to-Go I'd made sure that there *was* a back door.

The longship was already gone when I got outside, but I did find a pile of plastic trays lying in the weeds in the far corner of the parking lot.

The news that night was all about what the Talking Head called the Fast Food Massacres, but it was Thursday before I heard any mention of the Vikings themselves. A passerby saw them hit Hungry Burger, a little hole-in-the-wall right downtown, and described the longship, right down to the row of pizza pans hanging along the sides. She called them shields, but I'm here to tell you they were pizza pans. Nobody believed her but me, of course, but given the similarities with the massacre at Rickenbacker's she got a lot of attention.

She didn't call the raiders Vikings, which I suppose wasn't all that surprising. By now they were all wearing modern clothes: blue jeans or sweat pants, and sneakers, with coats or windbreakers over their armor. Only their helmets and weapons remained to identify them as Vikings; and one of them had a motorcycle helmet with a tinted visor, along with a complete set of black motorcycle leathers. I think he was their leader, the big one with the huge red mustache. I'm not sure, because I didn't take time to look carefully. As soon as I caught the wonderful sour smell of Eau de Viking I was down the passage to the back door and the alley where my bike was parked.

I have to say, I was getting really tired of not being able to eat my lunch in peace. Lunch out is one of my few luxuries, and I like to take my time over it. On top of that, I was perplexed and uneasy. The mere fact of Viking raiders was bad enough; but why were they following me around? I was beginning to feel like a jinx.

On Friday, I was at a bit of a loss. Corey's End is a fair-sized town, but it's not huge, and it was getting hard to pick a place worth eating at that I wouldn't miss if the Vikings torched it. On the other hand, I didn't like the idea of eating lunch at home, for fear that I'd have Vikings as surprise house guests.

I finally ended up at the lunch counter at Johansen's Department Store. They make an OK cheeseburger, and their real old-fashioned hand-scooped milkshakes are worth the extra ten minutes it takes me to ride there. I was finishing the last of my french fries (salty, and just crispy enough on the outside) when the door crashed open and the Vikings slammed into the room. This time I was ready for them. I had positioned myself at one end of the counter so that I could duck behind it at a moment's notice and then escape through the kitchen. Then the counter waitress, who had clearly been watching the same news stories as me and wasn't too happy about it, dropped a full pot of coffee on the faded green linoleum right at my feet. The combination of broken glass and scalding coffee brought me to an immediate halt, and there I was, stuck. I couldn't run, and there at the counter there was no place to hide. Plan C didn't bear thinking about. I figured I was a goner, but as it turned out the Vikings had bigger fish to fry.

Johansen's Department Store is an old brick building from the 1950's. The lunch counter is in a kind of bay at one end. It has its own outside door on one side, and is open to the rest of the store on the other. The Vikings came in, ready for some petty theft with an order of bloodshed on the side—and then froze as they caught sight of the cornucopia of excellent goods at low prices that is Johansen's, all waiting for them just beyond the row of stools. They all looked at each other, and back at the riches of American commerce. They lowered their axes and huddled together for a quick conference, punctuated by expansive gestures and the occasional glance at the merchandise. It ended with a roar of laughing approval, during which they shook their axes in the air; then, all but two of them moved further into the store. They never so much as looked at me and the other customers. One Viking headed back outside to the longship...and to my surprise and wonder set it on fire. It was burning merrily by the time the police showed up.

The last Viking was Red Mustache, resplendent in his motorcycle helmet and leathers. I watched him, holding onto my stool for dear life so as not to fall into the puddle of glass and coffee, and he just stood there, shoulders slumped. He looked from under his raised visor at the Viking committing arson in the parking lot, and then at the Vikings committing grand theft in the department store, and then back again. After a while he took a long breath and shook his head. I got a good look at his face. Behind his mustache he looked like he'd bitten into something rotten and was only half-surprised. Then he followed his compatriots further into the store.

I couldn't understand the Viking's language, of course, but afterwards I was nearly certain I could reconstruct their little conference:

Big Nose: Hey, look at all the neat stuff these people have got!

Blond Braid: And they don't seem able to fight, at all, at all.

Fringe Beard: No, they just look surprised when you hit them, and then they fall over.

Big Nose: Does anyone see any reason why we shouldn't just stay here? We'll be ruling the roost in a matter of days!

All: General shout of approval!

I'm sure there was a similar confab on the shores of England when the first Danes landed in the 9th century:

Big Nose: Hey, look at the weather these people have!

Blond Braid: Yeah, it's not always freezing here.

Fringe Beard: And look at all the farm land.   Why, there's acres of it just lying there, under all of these dead people.

Blond Braid: Good fertilizer, that.

Big Nose: Does anyone see any reason why we shouldn't just stay here? We'll be ruling the roost in a matter of days!

All: General shout of approval!

(I'd read up on the Vikings since Monday.)

It would have been worth a few chuckles to watch the Vikings roam about the store, drooling over chef's knives, wrapping themselves up in down comforters, puzzling over the store's varied collection of pliers and socket wrenches, and goggling at assorted other goods. I saw one struck dumb with a mixture of admiration and horror at the mannikins at the entrance to Women's Wear, that was a laugh. But I cut away home as soon as the police showed up. I don't like dealing with the police; whenever I have a chat with them the conversation always goes the same way:

Cop: Hey, kid, are you all right?

Me: Yes, I'm fine.

Cop: What's your name, kid?

Me: Michael.

Cop: Mikey, huh?

Me: I prefer Michael.

Cop: Well, Mikey, are your parents here?

Me: That would be no.

The conversation spirals down from there, hitting bottom when I pull out my state ID card.

Cop: What's this?

Me: My ID.

Cop: Like hell it is.

Me: It's not a fake. I'm just small for my age.

Cop: Mikey, do you know what the penalty is for carrying a fake ID?

And that leads into another twenty minutes or so of wrangling.

Sometimes I have to call my landlady to vouch for me. It just isn't worth it. So I went home and waited to see the highlights on KCE.

I have to say, it didn't work out the way I'd figured. The Vikings didn't attack anyone at Johansen's, and nobody but me had really seen them in action earlier in the week. Well, not for long enough to matter. So the police arrested them on the basis of the battle axes they were hauling around with them, and I think on a charge of arson. Somehow they managed to make it stick without bloodshed, though one of the mannikins at the entrance to Women's Wear was a casualty of gun fire. The Vikings hadn't seen guns before, and had been inclined not to take them seriously. (Afterward they viewed them with respect and a wild surmise, along with much calculation and several heaping dollops of greed.)

So they were arrested all right, but there was no eyewitness testimony as to their crimes, except for setting the longship on fire; and then, as the cops were loading Red Mustache and his companions into the squad cars the longship vanished, flames and all. The Vikings' battle axes, armor, and helmets vanished too, leaving an empty spot in the middle of the physical evidence. I still don't know how Red Mustache did it, and I really wish I knew; it would have spared me quite a lot of trouble later on. "Useful" doesn't begin to describe it.

The cops were nonplussed, and Charlie Johansen was so taken with the thought of really truly Vikings coming across the ages just to raid his very own store that he paid their bail and brought them home to dinner. He's a Viking wannabe, is our Charlie, one of those re-enactor types. I later heard that he offered them lutefisk, and other Scandinavian delicacies, but what they really wanted was pizza. Rickenbacker's was still closed, which served them right.

All in all, it was quite a week.

Chapter 2

Nothing much happened over the weekend. The Vikings were out of commission, having burnt their boat behind them, and so I managed to eat lunch without worrying about being disturbed by death and mayhem. I ate it at home, alas. What I really wanted to do was get out and look around, do a little listening here and there. I was dying to find out if any of Charlie Johansen's re-enactor buddies were nutty enough to have studied the Viking lingo, ancient Scandawegian or whatever it was, and if so whether they could talk with the Red Mustache Gang. A cold front moved in overnight, though, and the rain kept me at home. My bike's handy for getting around town unnoticed—who pays attention to a small person on a bike? But that only works when the conditions are right. I can't ride around late at night, or in bad weather, without some officious Person of Size stopping to offer me a ride or ask what in hell I'm doing out so late. Riding a bike in the rain is no fun anyway. I thought about getting a car once, but when you're small for your age, driving a car gets you noticed double quick. Have I mentioned that I don't like talking to cops?

So I stayed in, drank hot chocolate, and got a little work done. I don't usually work on weekends, but I was behind, having been somewhat distracted by the events of the week. In between tasks I watched the rain puddle in the driveway and thought about the Vikings.

What do I do? You might call me a wizard-for-hire. I design long, intricate incantations that do the wondrous things that make our civilization function—which is to say that I'm a freelance software developer. These days it's mostly web development, but I'll try my hand at pretty much anything. If work is slow, there's always more to learn...and that opens up opportunities for future work. The important thing is that I can do all of the work I need to do from the comfort of my apartment, earning myself a tidy living without having to be face-to-face with giants. 'Nuff said.

So that was Saturday. On Sunday I watched some more rain, and I did some more work, and then I splashed down the outside stairs and across the driveway to have dinner with Mrs. Henderson, my landlady. She can call me Mikey if she likes; but don't *you* try it.

By Monday morning the rain had stopped, and I began to feel like I was being watched. I didn't like it.

I'd worked diligently all morning on an order-entry system for some guy in Duluth. At lunch time I headed back to Johansen's Department Store. Dino's had burned to the ground, and the other joints were all still out of commission, and anyway I thought I might hear some gossip about Charlie's house guests while sipping a chocolate shake at the lunch counter. It was on the way there that I began to get a creepy feeling between my shoulder blades. When you're small for your age you learn to pay attention to feelings like that.

The useful thing about riding a bicycle is that you can go places cars can't, and you can outrun most anybody on foot. I made a judicious change in my route, turning down a narrow path between two buildings, and the feeling vanished...only to return full force while I was sitting at the lunch counter waiting for my food. This is a basic problem with lunch counters: you sit with your back to the room, and you can't scope out the place, casual-like, without alerting anyone who is watching. I could have sat in a booth, but a small person sitting by himself in a booth never gets any service: the waitress always figures that Mom or Dad will be along soon, and she'd rather deal with them. I really did want to eat, so I sat at the counter.

If Charlie's father had installed a mirror on the wall behind the counter, like they have behind the bar in all those old westerns, I'd have been golden. Instead, there was a big menu board—informative, but not at all reflective, and so not particularly revealing. I fiddled with my silverware trying to get a decent reflection in my spoon, but all I could see was my own face, bulging like a bullfrog. And you can't just turn around and look, because that lets them know you know, so I had to just sit there and take it. I hate that.

I tried to tell myself that there was nothing much interesting in watching a small person eating a cheeseburger and fries at the lunch counter, and that my observer would soon get bored and move on. In the meantime I kept my ears open.

"Wasn't that something, Stella, when those guys came in the other day?"

The voice was deep and a bit creaky, and it was attached to an older guy a few stools down. He had a feed cap and a pot belly, and looked like a retired truck-driver. He'd pushed his plate out of the way and was hunched over his belly with his elbows on the counter.

"Sure was," said the waitress, she who had dropped the pot of coffee and ruined my bolt hole. She'd never apologized for that, either. At least, not to me.

"Were you here when it happened?"

"That I was," she said, putting a cup of coffee in front of him. "You want cream, it's right there," she said. The guy couldn't take a hint, though.

"No, thanks, my wife'd kill me. Cholesterol. Who were they, anyway? Didja ever find out?"

"Vikings, I guess. But you'd have to ask Mr. Johansen about that," she said, and busied herself refilling cups of coffee and other such waitress-like chores. She clearly didn't want to talk about it. I scowled, and settled down to enjoy my milkshake as best I could with somebody's eyeballs boring a hole in my spine.

When I was done I left some cash on the counter for Stella the coffee-pot-dropper. I always pay cash; ATMs don't ask you what you're doing with your father's credit card. I scanned the room casually as I got up, but nobody seemed to be paying any attention to me, either at the lunch counter or in the booths behind it, or out in the store itself.

The feeling had gone away by the time I'd unlocked my bike, but I took a circuitous route through Corey Park and down several alleys just in case.

The feeling of being watched persisted all day Tuesday, at least while I was out and about. I kept my eyes open, but was never able to figure who it was that was following me. There were two interesting bits of news involving the Vikings, though. First, Johansen's Department Store ran a full page ad in the *Town Crier*, featuring a picture of Fringe Beard and Blond Braid in full Viking regalia. Fringe Beard was lolling on a bed surrounded by merchandise of every kind while Blond Braid stood by and looked fierce. The regalia looked to have come from a costumer's, and was even further over the top than the gear they'd had at Dino's. They looked like a pair of Texas longhorns: *Thor Rides Again*. It was a pity their own gear had vanished with the longship; it had looked a lot more functional, and had certainly fit better.

Oddly, it didn't seem to have been any more authentic. While reading up on Vikings, I'd learned that they wore leather helmets, or metal if they were wealthy, and most definitely without horns. Some few had iron swords, but mostly they carried spears, and wooden shields. Battle axes were no more typical than AK47's.

Historically accurate or not, though, the Red Mustache Gang had both looked and been deadly when they stormed into Dino's. Now they just looked silly.

The other news item involved the Vikings' appearance in court, what they call an arraignment. It seems that one of

Charlie Johansen's re-enactor buddies was both a lawyer and a nut who rejoiced in reading ancient Viking poetry in the original language. (You'd think he'd want to take a break from obscure, archaic formalisms after hours, but apparently not.) (But then, who am I to talk? I'm a software guy. I rejoice in obscure, modernistic formalisms.) He'd managed to communicate with our guests from yesteryear, if a bit haltingly, as witness Exhibit A: to wit, the full page ad in the *Town Crier*. In addition, he was representing them in court.

But although this was interesting to me personally, as I still wanted to know what in hell the Red Mustache Gang was doing in my town, and why they had been following me about, and it would be helpful if I could, you know, *ask* them, the bottom of the article was more interesting. It included a description of Red Mustache, the alleged leader of the gang, and said that he had run for it. Skipped town. Flown the coop. (I had a momentary vision of him taking to the air with great flaps of his enormous red mustachios.) In short, no one, least of all the other members of his gang, had any idea where he was. It sounded suspicious to me, and evidently Judge Walker felt the same; and our Charlie had to forfeit some of his bail money.

By Wednesday the rain was threatening again, and I went to the grocery store for supplies. I usually do my shopping on Fridays, but not only do I hate to ride my bike in the rain, I doubly hate trying to shlep groceries home on my bike in the rain. (The sourdough bread always gets soggy.) Once I got caught short by a storm that blew in early Friday morning, and I was stuck in the house for a week. I spent the last several days living on water and Cheerios.

Well, I would have if it hadn't been for Mrs. Henderson.

Anyway, when the Mongol hordes arrived I was at Foodland, stocking up on Cheerios, trying to keep an eye out for watchers, and resisting the urge to scratch between my shoulder blades in public. There was a loud clattering noise from the front of the store, and I when I looked down the aisle, well....

If you've never seen a little guy on a shaggy pony come barreling down Aisle 5 with a sword poised to carve out your liver and lights, take it from me that it's a galvanizing experience. Took me straight back to middle school, it did. Aisle 5 is the canned food aisle, and the moment I saw the flash of the sword I was climbing up the shelves past the Campbell's Cream of Mushroom like a monkey—a creature I do not otherwise resemble. I might be small for my age, but I'm not funny-looking.

Once I reached the top I draped myself over the divider between Aisles 5 and 6 (soft drinks, if you're interested), and thanked my lucky stars I hadn't been looking at frozen pizza. I wasn't comfortable, but I wasn't dead, either.

The Mongol hordes—well, there were maybe a dozen of them, all on ponies, all with fiendish grins and long black mustaches and shaggy fur hats that made them look like their ponies—the Mongol hordes did not stick around for long. They hit the butcher's counter for raw steaks, which they stashed under their saddles, and also picked up quite a selection of chips, bean dip, and imported beer. Oh, and Hershey bars, the great big ones. Then they were off through the automatic doors, and vanished before they were all of the way across the parking lot. Neat trick, that. They never got down from their ponies, so the shoppers with the presence of mind to seek higher ground came through the attack OK; those who stayed down on the floor...didn't.

I waited a good five minutes before climbing down and collecting my cart, which I steered carefully and circuitously to the front of the store. Judging that the surviving checkers were going to be in hysterics for at least another half-hour (and who can blame them?) I bagged my stuff as quickly as I could and left the cash on the counter. The Roman Legions were about due, by my calculations, and I wanted to be sure to miss them.

On my way to the exit I saw a giantess climbing out from underneath the manager's desk. I was right in her field of view as she got to her feet, and she stared at me, hand to her mouth.

She wasn't wearing a Foodland uniform, so she wasn't the manager, just another customer. I nodded at her approvingly— she wasn't having hysterics, and she got points for finding good cover at ground level—and her eyes widened. Blonde bangs, but dark eyebrows...an odd combination. I couldn't think why she was staring at me, with so much else of interest in all directions. I didn't spend much time on it, though. I was too angry with the Mongols to think about anything else.

Thursday afternoon was when the trouble started. I was hard at work, minding my own business, when some officious busybody knocked on the door of my apartment. I hate it when that happens.

Maybe you've gotten the idea that I don't like people. That's not true. I find people endlessly fascinating. I can sit and watch them for hours. After all, that's what YouTube is for. What I hate is being bothered while I'm working. Or eating. Or...not working.

Anyway, I grabbed the stool I keep by the door and took a look through the fisheye. There was some giantess on the landing. I got down, moved the stool out of the way, and opened the door a crack.

"Yeah?"

The giantess peered down through the crack at me. I saw a dark eyebrow and a touch of blonde hair. That should have tipped me off, but my head was full of database table schemas and source code, and I wanted to keep it that way.

"Are you Michael Henderson?" she said.

"Yeah. What do you want?" Rude, I know. Sorry.

Instead of answering she shoved the door open, pushing me out of the way and knocking over the stool. I lost my balance, and fell on my—I lost my balance. I wasn't expecting it, and hadn't braced myself for it; and it probably wouldn't have mattered if I had. The giantess must have been at least five-foot eleven, and she outweighed me by quite a bit. She closed the door, and backed away from me, towards the kitchen door.

"Go over there. Go sit down over there," she said as I picked myself up. She sounded nervous. She was also, I noticed, pulling a pistol out of her handbag. I don't know what kind it was. It was black, and not too big—for her, anyway—but she didn't seem comfortable with it. There's no profit in arguing with crazy people with guns, so I backed away from her and sat down on the edge of the couch like a good little boy.

"What is this?" I said, staring at the pistol. "And could you please put that thing away? It makes me nervous."

"You were there," she said, moving to the center of the room. The bore of the gun stayed pointed more or less in my direction, but I noticed it was moving around a lot. Her hands were shaking. I wondered if the gun was loaded, and decided not to find out.

When you're pinned down, bluster.

"I was there? What there? When? Who the hell are you?" I was getting tired of looking at the pistol, so I looked at her face instead. She was younger than I'd realized, probably about my own age. Her face was screwed up in a frown, but I thought she might be kind of cute if she weren't scared to death. Well, for a giantess. But what on earth was she scared of? The gun? It couldn't be me. I'm about as scary as a plush toy.

Those eyebrows...where had I seen eyebrows like hers?

"At Hungry Burger," she said. "You were there. I saw you come out after they...after they left."

Oooooooh, I thought. The news report hadn't said who the eye-witness was, but I thought I could put a face to her.

"And at Rickenbacker's. And all of the other places. And then today, you were at Foodland." She took a deep breath, and I finally placed her. She was the one who had hidden behind the manager's desk, the one who had stared at me as I left. I began to think I'd found my watcher. I stared at her harder, and she started to sob. "You were there, every time, and they died, they all died! How could you? What's the matter with you! *How could you?*"

She eased her grip on the gun when the waterworks started,

but as her voice got louder she seemed to remember it again, and I decided it was time for Plan C. She'd kept her distance, but it's a small room. I'd kept my feet under me and my weight forward, and as the gun started to come up I launched myself straight for her knees. I may be small, but I'm an expert in applied leverage. The gun went off as she toppled over my back. The sound was shocking, and so was the smell, but momentum carried me forward.

In school I always tried to be unavailable rather than face frontal assaults, but there were occasions when I learned that the best defense really is a good offense. She'd gone down on all fours, and the moment I was up I leaped onto her back. She went down the rest of the way, gasping as the wind went out of her, and lost her grip on the gun. I swarmed over her head, grabbed the gun, and slid it across the floor and under the couch. There was a muffled thump as it hit the wall. Then I climbed off of her. She didn't seem dangerous, now that I'd disarmed her, and anyway I still didn't understand what her problem was. It's not like I was the one who had killed all of those people. So I went and sat back down on the couch, and waited for her to get up.

That might sound cold-blooded, and I wouldn't want you to think that I was relaxed about being shot at. Normally I'd have been moving away at speed after something like this. But there are basic facts of my existence, and there was no point in going anywhere until they'd all played out.

Mystery Girl surprised me, though: she didn't get up. She just lay there on the floor, crying her eyes out. I studied her from where I sat; nothing appeared to be broken, and I hadn't hit her that hard. Stress; some people just can't handle it. Or maybe it was frustration. Or, maybe...well, I gave up. I'd never been able to understand girls.

Meanwhile, I was counting quietly under my breath. Before I reached eight I heard steps hurrying up the stairs toward my front door. The moment I reached ten, my door swung open and my landlady appeared, worry written all over her face.

"Mikey, are you all right? What happened? Was that a gunshot?" Then she saw the giantess sobbing on my floor.

"Hi, Mom," I said.

Like I said, it was on Thursday afternoon that the trouble started.

Chapter 3

Okay, okay. So I'm an anti-social twenty-something computer geek who lives with his mom. At least I don't live in the basement. I've got my own apartment over the garage, I've got my own front door, I prepare my own meals (except for Sunday dinner) and I'm self-supporting. So I call her my landlady. Wouldn't you, in my position? So sue me. I can afford it.

It was interesting watching the play of emotions on Mom's face: first, the fear and concern that brought her running, followed by pleasure that I had a visitor—and a girl, at that—followed by anger and concern when she realized that I was OK and the girl was sobbing on the floor, followed by a stern glare as she shepherded the young lady out the door that said I'd damn well better be there when she came back.

After she left, I tried to assess the damage. There was a neat black hole in the fake wood paneling, just above the back of the couch, just about the level my head would have been at while I was sitting. When I saw it, I had to sit down again—but not on the couch. Then I had to go into the bathroom and look at the top of my head in the mirror, just to verify that the bullet hadn't parted my hair. Then I went back into the living room and propped a throw pillow on the back of the couch, just in front of the hole, and opened the windows so that the smell of cordite would dissipate. I left the gun where it was, under the couch.

Then I began to wonder where the bullet was. The paneling

isn't that thick. I went around the corner and looked at the other side of the wall, where I keep a floor-to-ceiling bookcase filled with software texts and reference manuals. There was no sign of damage, but I suspected that one of the volumes had taken a bullet in my place. At a guess, it was one of the tomes in the middle of the Microsoft Windows section, in which case it couldn't happen to a nicer book. I'd have to look for it later, but first I had to go and sit down some more.

I was still sitting when I heard Mom coming back up the stairs, though by this time I'd gotten a bottle of Newcastle Brown from the refrigerator. I don't often drink beer, mostly because what I have to go through to buy it is so humiliating, but I try to have some on hand for special occasions. This occasion wasn't particularly special, but on the other hand I had never been shot at before. I felt I needed some relaxing.

Mom came in without knocking, closed the door, and planted her feet. She's got this look, and she used it without stinting. You know the one: head down, looking at you from under her brows.

"Michael, what did you do to that nice young woman?"

"You mean the walking puddle?"

"Michael." She crossed her arms. The eyes, they kept looking.

"I didn't do anything to her, Mom."

She raised an eyebrow. The arms, they remained crossed.

"I swear, Mom, I don't even know who she is. She got here just a couple of minutes before you came in."

"So, she just waltzed in and collapsed in a heap on your living room carpet, crying her eyes out."

"Well, more or less, yes, that's what happened."

The eyebrow, it remained raised. The arms, they remained crossed. The demeanor, it remained disbelieving.

Then the other eyebrow went up.

Time passed. One of the great masters might have titled it, "Still life, with Accusation." They say that great art always evokes a response from the viewer. In my case, I squirmed a bit.

"She was already upset when she got here, Mom."

No change. I tried again.

"She seemed to think I had something to do with the Viking attacks. I dunno, maybe someone she knows was killed."

An eyebrow came down, which should have been an improvement but wasn't. It just emphasized the other one. Then she made that little twirly "get on with it" motion with her right hand. At least her arms weren't crossed any more.

"She saw me coming out of Dino's the day it burned down."

That got her attention. Her brow came down, her eyelids went up, and without taking her eyes off of me for a moment she dropped into the overstuffed chair across from me. I don't think she was really seeing me, though.

"I thought that was just a fire," she said.

"No, it was the Vikings."

I gave her a capsule summary of the occasion, leaving out the gory bits. I didn't say anything about my subsequent encounters with Red Mustache and his crew. Or about the Mongols, for that matter. No doubt she'd hear about the Mongols soon enough.

"Why didn't you tell me?"

"What was there to tell? I wasn't hurt, and anyway, who'd have believed me?"

"But you could have been killed!"

I looked down, hoping that she wasn't going to leap across the room and smother me like she used to do when I was twelve and came home with a black eye.

After that it got soppy for a bit. You'll pardon me if I don't go into detail. Then, just as I'd begun to hope that she'd forgotten about Mystery Girl, Mom asked, "But why does she think you're involved?"

"I dunno," I lied. "All she managed to say was, 'How could you?'" I harrumphed a bit. "Like I'd torch Dino's. Anyone who knows me knows I would never do that."

Mom had to nod at that. She knows how much I loved Dino's.

"Did she give you her name?"

"No, she didn't," Mom said. "She just drank the hot chocolate I made for her, thanked me, and drove off."

"Humph," I said. "Well, as sorry as I am not to be introducing you to your future daughter-in-law, it's the middle of my day. I've got to get back to work."

She glanced at the bottle I was holding. "Do you always drink beer when you're working?"

"Special occasion," I said. I didn't elaborate.

Mom nodded, and got up. On the way out the door she turned and said, "You've got to go talk to the police, you know." Then she glided down the stairs.

You'll have noticed that I didn't mention the pistol, or the bullet hole in my wall. So why didn't I tell Mom the whole story, tell her how that "nice young woman" had pulled a gun on me and had nearly vitiated my future career in the most permanent possible way?

I'm not sure. Part of it is that I was certain that Mom already knew. Mom's no idiot. She hears a gunshot, she smells the cordite, she finds an otherwise unhurt girl on the floor...what's she supposed to think? She knows *I* didn't pull the trigger. Hence her questions. She was really asking why such a nice girl would want to shoot me. It's one of the things I love about Mom —over the years she's learned not to be over-protective.

But mostly, I think, I kept quiet because Mystery Girl had a legitimate beef. It wasn't with me, really, but she thought it was. It's kind of refreshing to have someone after me for something they think I've done, instead of for no particular reason, the way it usually is. And then, Mystery Girl had clearly been *in extremis*. She'd been under stress, she had a gun she didn't know how to use and was afraid of, and I don't think she'd really meant to shoot me. She had a question, and she wanted the answer. "How could you?" she'd asked. And I wanted to know the answer to that myself.

The rest of the week was quiet, with no more Mongol attacks. I stayed at home, tending to my work and avoiding both fast food joints and grocery stores. Mystery Girl didn't come back. I patched the hole in my wall, and touched it up with the leftover paint from the shelf in the garage. Did a pretty good job, if I do say so myself. You, you'll have to take my word for it. I had a subdued dinner with Mom on Sunday; she didn't mention the police, and I didn't go talk to them. But I did a lot of thinking. And thus it was that Monday morning found me out shopping again.

To be specific, I went to #1 Fine Market to buy a sack of Chinese rice. #1 Fine Market is one of the few ethnic grocery stores in Corey's End. I don't shop there very often—the prices aren't marked in English, and I'm morally certain Mr. Lee raises the price for white folk. He's short-changed me a time or two as well. To give credit where credit is due, I don't think it has anything to do with my height. This, as I've indicated before, is refreshing, but it isn't endearing.

I found the rice easily enough—the white sacks stand out, even in the dim light—and after casting about a bit managed to locate one of the rare five-pound sacks. The thirty-pound sacks are simply out of my weight class, either to carry or to consume. Then I mooched slowly around the store, studying the packages and guessing whether their contents were, in fact, edible, while I waited for the Mongols to show up. Assuming they were going to.

I felt a little bad bringing down the Mongol hordes on Mr. Lee's grocery store, though I can't deny that there was a certain historical beauty to it. (I'd read up on the Mongols, too.) Truly, it had nothing to do with Mr. Lee's prices or pecuniary sleight-of-hand. Almost nothing; I'm not usually the vengeful sort. When you're small for your age, you can't afford to be. No, mostly it had to do with Mr. Lee's aisles.

See, the #1 Fine Market is a tiny little place, tucked in between a dry cleaners and one of those no-name pizza delivery places that somehow manages to survive even though no one ever buys pizza there. I've always figured they launder clothes on one side and money on the other. But I digress.

The point is, the aisles at the #1 Fine Market are only about three feet wide. That's just enough space for one shopper with a shopping cart to pass through—except that they can't, because every aisle usually has a stack of ideogram-encrusted boxes running down the middle. Me, I can just squeak through on one side or the other. How other shoppers manage I don't know, but that hardly matters as I've never seen any.

I didn't have to wait long. I was studying a package of dried noodles—at least, I think they were noodles, though it might have been a product for scrubbing dishes—when the first Mongol rider charged in through the door and had to immediately rein up to avoid crashing into the counter where Mr. Lee presides with his ancient cash register. Mr. Lee dropped behind the counter like a stone. He's a survivor of the Cultural Revolution, and he can read the writing on the walls all by himself, thank you very much. There are no flies on Mr. Lee, which is more than I can say for his fish counter.

The rider turned his horse to the left, and then right again, and charged down my aisle, where his pony reared and lost its footing on the faded linoleum floor, sliding rear hoofs first into the Great Wall of Boxes. The pony went down in a cascade of rice, cans of water chestnut, bags of dried mushrooms, bottles of soy and plum sauce, and sundry other goods I don't even know the names of, before coming down on top of its rider. He cursed in shock and pain, and his pony screamed—an awful noise— while the other riders milled about the parking lot in confusion, trying to see in through the dirty plate glass.

I didn't try to get a good look at them, or wait to see what they did next. I had what I'd come for, and I don't mean groceries. Leaving the as-yet-unpurchased bag of rice on the floor, I slipped out the delivery door and hid behind the dumpster until I was sure they had gone. Then I collected my bike, which I'd left chained to a fence around the corner, and pedaled on home.

Well, that tore it. The Mongols *were* following me around, just like the Vikings had. And now that I'd verified it, what was I going to do for groceries? I couldn't go back to Foodland, not after what had happened there the last time. Could I order groceries on-line? And what would happen to the delivery van if

I did? Did a delivery van count as a grocery store to whatever intelligence was responsible for delivering ancient marauders into my lap? It seemed a bit inconsiderate to call the Mongol hordes down on an unsuspecting delivery van driver.

It was some small consolation that at least I could go out to eat safely; the Vikings had been defanged, as it were, and were no longer a problem. But I couldn't eat out forever.

I did not go to sleep with a peaceful mind.

Although no one was hurt (except for the one Mongol and his pony, who did not stick around to be counted) the second Mongol raid did not go unnoticed, and when I ventured out on Wednesday the spot between my shoulder blades was itching again. It was Mystery Girl, of course. She was trying to be surreptitious about it, but now that I knew what she looked like it wasn't much use. I've got one of those little rear-view mirrors attached to my bicycle helmet, and I several times caught sight of her behind me.

I led her and her eyebrows all over town, just for for spite, until I got bored with it and stopped for dinner at the Pancake Hut (known unofficially to all and sundry as the Local House of Pancakes, or LHOP). By then she'd figured out that I knew she was following me, so she didn't try to hide; instead, she quite deliberately asked the hostess for a table about ten feet in front of me where I couldn't help seeing her and she could glare at me over her scrambled eggs and french toast. It rather put me off my food, but I did my best to ignore her with the help of a thriller I'd loaded onto my phone. When you eat alone all the time, a novel is good company. Usually, it's good company. That night I just couldn't focus on it.

And so there we sat, just like that, her glaring and me pretending to read, and me beginning to think that maybe I should go sit down at her table and have it out with her, and her lowering those brows at me, and me wondering whether she'd collapse in tears again if I did, and her snarling at me, if you can snarl with a mouthful of french toast, and me trying to ignore her, when so help me a Roman Legion surrounded the place and locked it up tighter than a bank vault.

Chapter 4

I call it a Roman Legion; there were really only about sixty of them, which would make up what they called a century, a small fraction of a full legion. (I boned up on the Romans, too, but that was later.) You'd think a century would be a hundred men, but apparently not. They were wearing those breastplates and funny armored skirt things, like in the movies, and they smelled—but not like the Mongols. It was a cleaner smell, and somehow a temporary one; I got the sense that yeah, they'd been out in the field for a while, but they'd get cleaned up as soon as they had the chance.

I have to say, those Romans were a class act. There was none of your charging about the restaurant bellowing and chopping people in two and leaving puddles of blood everywhere, as I'd seen so often in the previous couple of weeks. There was no looting, either. Instead, a squad of largish men with drawn short swords came in and made it clear with a few choice if unintelligible phrases that there was to be no nonsense—not that any of us were contemplating any such thing—and then herded all of us, including the waitresses and cooks, into one corner. I found myself pushed up against a window, where I saw that the rest of the legionaries were outside setting up a perimeter. A number of the other customers were sobbing or having hysterics, but I did my best to ignore them. This was easier than you might think; on-going shrieks turn out to be easier to cope with, emotionally speaking, than shrieks that are suddenly cut off in mid-cry.

The LHOP is kind of off by itself; it was supposed to be part of a larger shopping area, but the economy changed and the other stores were never built. There are vacant lots on three sides, all dirt and weeds and gravel, and in these the legionaries were industriously digging a ditch and turning the excavated earth into a palisade topped with pointed sticks. It made me wonder what they were doing on the fourth side, where the parking lot was, but I was at the back of the building and of course I couldn't see that.

I also began to wonder how long they were planning on staying, and whether they'd be following me around the way the Vikings and Mongols had, and under what conditions, when I was stopped in mid-ponder by a soft but cutting voice in my ear.

"This is all your doing. I hope you're satisfied."

It was Mystery Girl, of course; I recognized the tones of indignation and outrage. I didn't bother turning to look at her.

"I don't know how you figure that," I said, "but if I were responsible don't you think I'd be out there rather than in here?"

"I'm sure you're sorry you weren't able to manage it, this time."

I was trying to put together a good come-back when a shouted —okay, bellowed—order from our guards intervened. The original squad of men had been augmented by another, led by a guy who looked rather more flashy than the others. He wasn't as large as some of them, but he stood even more upright. From the way the others deferred to him I gathered that he was the man in charge, what they call a centurion. I knew that word from old movies, and hoped it was the right one. Anyway, at a word from him two of the legionaries approached us and began separating the men from the women by the simple expedient of grabbing individuals one at a time and pushing them roughly (but not viciously) to one side or the other. No one made any trouble until one of the legionaries, a big guy with a broken nose and a bored expression, got around to Mystery Girl. She had her right hand in her purse, and when he grabbed her by her left arm, her right hand emerged clutching a small tube.

It was mace. Me being next to her, I got just enough of a whiff to be glad that she hadn't had the opportunity to use it on me. Old Broken Nose, he wasn't so lucky. He got it right in the eyes, as Mystery Girl hollered, "Got you, you murdering bastard!" Which was hardly fair, if you think about it. The Romans hadn't killed anybody yet, so far as I knew. Well, not in Corey's End, anyway.

I don't know what Mystery Girl was trying to accomplish, but whatever it was, it didn't work. No sooner was Broken Nose staggering about than one of his mates clubbed her to the ground with the flat of his short sword.

She was still limp when the sorting was complete. One of the legionaries picked her up and carried her out of the room like a sack of potatoes, the other women following behind at sword point. Several of the men looked like they wanted to object, but Broken Nose's buddy looked like he'd welcome a chance to do some more clubbing, with maybe a stab or two throw in, so things remained peaceful.

That left all of us men huddled sullenly in the corner...or, rather, all of the men and me, for Mr. Centurion hailed me, and jerked his head to indicate that I should follow him. He called me something like "poo-air", which probably wasn't meant to be as insulting as it sounded. He led me a little apart from the other captives, and then said, clearly, "*Aqua?*" He mimed drinking something.

I began to get the idea. Grab a boy; he'll think soldiers are cool. He'll tell us anything, and he's too little to be much of a problem. Plus, we left all of our camp followers behind, and we need a gofer. I just shrugged and pointed at one of the water glasses left behind on a table. He shook his head, and mimed pouring into the glass. Aha. He wanted to know where the water came from. I led him into the kitchen, grabbed a plastic water pitcher, and filled it up from the tap in one of the sinks.

He was quite impressed, especially when I showed him the difference between the hot and cold water taps.

It occurred to me that while I was being useful, I might as well be extra useful and make us all a lot more comfortable. So I made "this way, this way" gestures, and led him to the men's room. He got the idea right quick there, too, after I gave a discreet demonstration, and I could just see the gears turning in his head. Water supply; food supply; no sanitation issues to worry about. Yes, Mr. Centurion was feeling better about the defensibility of his current location all the time. I didn't have the heart to tell him that the water and power could be cut off from outside his perimeter with no trouble at all. Or the vocabulary, of course.

After that, Mr. Centurion just led me around the kitchen for a while, pointing at things, and had me show him what everything did. I just grinned like an idiot and let him go on thinking I was twelve.

Finally, he pointed at an empty pitcher and waved his arm expansively, taking in the whole restaurant and its environs. Apparently I was to going to get to play Gunga Din. I pointed toward the door, and then back into the seating area. Do I bring water to the legionaries, or to the captives? He repeated my gestures, with a deliberate pause in between. Legionaries first; *then* captives. Suited me just fine; I'd get a look at what they were doing, and maybe I'd find out what had happened to Mystery Girl and the other women.

I didn't see any reason to bring water to so many men one pitcher at a time, so I commandeered a kitchen cart and hunted down Pancake Hut's largest stock pot. Mr. Centurion watched me carefully until he saw me start to fill the pot, and then left me to it.

The legionaries looked at me kind of funny when I came out pushing the cart, but their attitudes changed really quickly when they realized I was bringing water. I kept my eyes open as I worked, and I noticed a number of interesting sights, none of which I could investigate in more detail without attracting attention. There was a variety of Roman gear stacked neatly behind the restaurant, for example; and lying near the back door there was a dead body. Oddly, the body was wearing neither legionary gear nor modern American clothing, but something I pegged as Roman civvies.

I went down the line filling helmets with water and running back and forth to the cart to refill my pitcher, and all the while I studied the palisade they'd built. It looked fairly solid, for a dirt wall, and it was tall enough that I couldn't see over it. I rather thought I could climb it, given a running start, and I could certainly wiggle through the pointed sticks with which they'd lined the top—but not while these eager beavers were standing about. I'd get about halfway up before one of them grabbed me and turned me over to Mr. Centurion.

When you're small for your age, you don't go looking for that kind of trouble.

I had to refill the stock pot of couple of times, and then I moved around to the parking lot in front of the Pancake Hut, which I'd purposely left for last. There, as I'd guessed, the legionaries had been unable to dig their usual trench or build their usual wall.

You know, those Romans were impressing me more and more. Unable to dig, they'd nevertheless built a stout barricade all along that side of the property using available materials—which is to say, the cars parked in the lot. They hadn't been any too gentle, either, and I winced at the scratches in the side of Mr. McGillicuddy's prize '65 Corvette. Joe McGillicuddy had taught me history when I was in high school. He was a good teacher, and he had style. He walked with a kind of loose swagger that I much admired, even after I learned that it was because of an injury he had gotten while serving with the Marines. The whole school had known that Mr. McGillicuddy's Corvette was his pride and joy.

Other than that, I was pleased by what I saw. The linchpin of the entire assembly was a bright yellow Hummer H2 they'd been unable to move from its spot...and as I have reason to know, I can crawl under an H2 like greased lightning.

I confess, I was tempted to execute Plan A right then and there. The legionaries were taking me more or less for granted by then, and I'd have had no trouble sliding under the Hummer. I might have gotten stuck with a javelin in the back for my troubles once I came out from under, but I've got a lot of experience at running away, and anyway it was starting to get dark. On the whole I thought my chances were pretty good.

It was the thought of Mystery Girl and the other women that stopped me. I still didn't know what had happened to them, and I was still smarting from Mystery Girl's contemptuous remarks. If I ran away it would confirm everything she'd been thinking about me, and I couldn't bear to give her the satisfaction. So I wheeled the cart back into the restaurant to bring water to the thirsty and visit the imprisoned. If Mystery Girl was woozy from her clubbing, I might even get to comfort the sick. Triple play.

When I came back in, I found the cooks busily cooking pancakes and sausages under the supervision of several legionaries who were doing their level best to look severe and failing. Perhaps I'd get to bring food to the hungry as well, and be four-for-four.

I brought water to the male captives first, since they were in a corner of the seating area just outside the kitchen, and anyway I knew where they were.

Mr. McGillicuddy was in one corner. "Have you seen the women, Michael?" he asked me as I handed him a glass of water, keeping his voice down.

"Not yet," I said quietly. "I'm looking." I didn't say anything more, because the guards were beginning to pay attention, and, well, I didn't say anything more. I just finished pouring drinks, and moved on.

The seating area at the Pancake Hut is large and serpentine, so you can't see the whole thing at once. I pushed my makeshift water cart through the aisles, and made it all the way to the cash register without seeing anyone else. I was puzzled. The women weren't in the kitchen, and they weren't outside, and they weren't in the seating area; what on earth had the Romans done with them? I was trying to figure out whether or not to check the ladies' room when I heard a groan from behind the cash register counter. I peeked around it, and there, on the floor, was Mystery Girl. She was sitting propped up against the wall, and she didn't look happy. Her blonde hair hung over her face, but I thought her eyes were closed. Leather cords bound her wrists and ankles.

I pondered her for a moment, then trotted to the kitchen and got a short stack of pancakes from the cooks. On the way back I grabbed some napkins and silverware from an empty table. I put the food and utensils on the counter by the cash register, along with a pitcher of water. Mystery Girl would certainly be thirsty, and might well be hungry, and it gave me a plausible reason for being there should Mr. Centurion or his minions come looking. Then I climbed up and sat cross-legged on the counter next to the food. I didn't want to appear to be sneaking; sometimes the best place to hide is in plain sight.

I poured a glass of water for Mystery Girl and set it carefully beside me. It wouldn't do to spill it. Then I glanced down at the object of my errand of mercy. She was wasn't moving, and it wouldn't do for the pancakes to get cold. So I emptied the rest of the pitcher over Mystery Girl's head.

She woke up spluttering and not at all pleased, which seemed to be her usual state. She looked around wildly, not at all sure where she was.

"Up here," I said. "Want some pancakes?" I proffered a forkful of pancakes and syrup.

She glared at me, and then the irate look in her eyes...well, it wasn't replaced, exactly, I guess it was augmented by a dawning realization that her innards were in a state just this side of rebellion. She shook her head, and winced.

"Concussion," I said sagely. "Nasty. Try not to move your head too much." I put the fork on the plate.

She took a few deep breaths. "What's going on?" she said.

"The Romans have built a defensive position around the place, the men are being held captive in the back, and the cooks are making pancakes. Oh, and there's sausage, too."

"And they're letting you wander about. Of course." She dabbed at her eyes with a wet hand, trying to clear her vision.

"Here," I said, handing her a napkin. "Use this. Anyway, why shouldn't they? They think I'm about twelve, and star-struck with soldiers in armor. I showed them how to use the faucets and the flush toilets, and now I can do no wrong."

She wiped her face, and then sneered at me. "So you *are* working with them. I knew it. You're always where the blood is deepest. So go on, tell me, what have they done with the other women?"

That's gratitude for you. I looked down at her, wondering whether to get another pitcher of water. Instead, I picked up the fork and started eating her pancakes. Buttermilk. I'd kill for sourdough, but you take what you can get.

"Actually," I said, chewing, "I think they let them go." Mystery Girl did a double-take while I swallowed. "I've been all over the restaurant, and around the outside, bringing water to the Romans. No women. They could be in the ladies' room, I suppose, but I don't think it's big enough."

"Let them go?" She sounded confused. It might have been an after-effect of being knocked on the head...and then again it might not be.

I shrugged, and took another fork-full. "They aren't here," I said, around a mouthful of pancake. "Pity, you could have gone with them."

I looked out the window at the barricade of cars. They had to have let them go. The timing fit. They'd come and gotten the women just as they were finishing their barricade. Slip the women out through the gap, slide the final car into place, and there we were, snug as bugs in a rug. All of us guys, and Mystery Girl, who'd had the bad sense to mace the wrong guy and consequently couldn't walk away. Some people have all the luck.

"In fact," I continued, "They've been remarkably well-behaved. They haven't really hurt anybody."

"Except for me," she retorted.

"Well, yeah, and I don't blame them. 'Would you, could you, with some mace? Would you, could you, in his face?' I think you should be counting your blessings." She rubbed her head, but did not contest the point. "Oh, and I did see one dead body."

Horror and vindication slammed onto her face in equal measure, and then she winced again. Apparently the collision was painful.

"I knew it," she said. "Who was it?"

"That's the interesting part," I said. "I'm pretty sure I recognized him. You will, too. Wait a sec."

I hopped down from the counter, and grabbed a copy of the *Town Crier* from the neat stack on the table by the door. I climbed back up, and flipped through it until I found the page I wanted. I refolded the paper with that page showing, and handed it down.

"Him," I said. "Third from the left, in the motorcycle leathers."

Mystery Girl scowled at it, trying, I think, to get her eyes to focus. Then her eyes widened.

"But that's—" she began, when there was an angry holler from across the room. It was Mr. Centurion, come to break up our little party. I grabbed the paper, and went into my star-struck hero-worshipper routine. It galled me, but I did it.

"Mr. Centurion, Mr. Centurion," I said eagerly, "Look at this!" I pointed at the picture in the paper, and waved him over. "Look at this!"

He strode over, scowling—I'm not sure I'd ever seen anyone really *stride* until that moment—and snatched the paper from me. He studied the picture, and his eyes narrowed. He looked back at me, and then, grabbing my arm, he pulled me down off the counter. In moments, it seemed like, we were behind the restaurant standing over the dead man. Mr. Centurion looked back and forth between the picture and the man's face, shadowy in the light streaming out of the open back door. At last he grunted.

There were no two ways about it. The clothes were different, but even in the twilight it was plainly the same man—the same nose, the same cheek bones, the same ears, the same build. The same extravagant mustachios. The man in the Roman robes with the gaping wound in his belly was our old friend and erstwhile Viking Red Mustache. And here I'd thought that he couldn't possibly smell any worse.

Chapter 5

Mr. Centurion turned to face me, the copy of the *Town Crier* clutched in his fist and frustration written all over his face. He clearly wanted to question me about the words in the paper, and just as clearly had no idea how. I decided to help him as best I could. I pointed at the picture in the paper, and then at the body. I stuck my tongue out at it, and pretended to spit on it, and hit the palm of my hand with a clenched fist a couple of times. Then I sniffed loudly and turned my back on it. I briefly considered dropping my trousers and mooning the corpse, but decided that that would be overdoing it. Mr. Centurion grunted, and I think he got the idea that the Roman citizen formerly known as Red Mustache was no friend of ours. He handed me the paper, and we went back inside.

Once there, Mr. Centurion waved me off; apparently he had some things to think about. I toddled along back to the front of the restaurant, where Mystery Girl had maneuvered herself into a more comfortable seat in one of the booths. She had her elbows on the table, with her wrists raised in front of her and her hands clasped as though she were praying. Her wrists were still bound, of course, so it's not like there was much else she *could* do. She was slumped forward, resting her head on her hands.

"Yup," I said, taking a seat across from her. "No question, it's him. I guess the Romans didn't like him either." Mystery Girl raised her head as I continued, "What I really don't understand..."—I broke off for a moment, and retrieved the plate of pancakes from the counter—"...what I really don't understand, is where the police are. Pancakes?"

Mystery Girl sat up the rest of the way. She made a face, but nodded.

"OK."

"Seems like they should have been here by now, dontcha think?" I said, cutting a few bites worth out of the stack of pancakes. "The Romans showed up a couple of hours ago. Seems like one of the women they set loose would have called them."

"You didn't," she said. For a change, she wasn't sneering at me. She just sounded tired.

"No, I didn't," I said. "At first, I didn't think anyone would believe me. And then when I thought they'd probably believe me, it was all out in the open and didn't seem to matter anymore." I put the fork on the plate, and slid it across the table to her. "Sorry I can't do anything about your hands, but I doubt you want me to feed you."

Her eyes hardened, just for a moment. "Absolutely not," she said. It was not simply a statement of preference; it had the force of an imperial decree.

I nodded easily. "I thought not." Then I leaned forward, my own elbows on the table, and cupped my chin in my hands. "So would you mind telling me, pretty please, why you pulled a gun on me?"

Mystery Girl didn't say anything for a long while. I don't think she knew what to say, and anyway she was figuring out how to eat pancakes with her wrists tied together. It'd have been entertaining to watch if it hadn't looked so painful. Although she had full use of her fingers and thumbs, the motion of her arms was restricted, and her two hands got in each other's way. It was like she had one arm with eight fingers and two inconveniently placed thumbs that could go up and down all she liked but couldn't go side to side very well.

She tried holding the fork in one hand and then in the other, pointing up and then pointing down, neither of which worked. If she could get the fork into the pancakes she couldn't get the pancakes to her mouth, and if she could get the fork to her mouth she couldn't get it into the pancakes. Eventually she worked out how to spear a bite of pancake using one hand, and then pass the fork to the other hand, turning it around as she did so that she could eat it. It took a little effort and a fair amount of contortion, not to mention much wrinkling of those dark eyebrows of hers, but soon she was feeding herself like a champ. Not a quitter, our Mystery Girl, but I already knew that. There was a bit of bulldog in her make up, if not in her appearance.

She ate a few bites, chewing them carefully. Then she spoke.

"Is there anything to drink?"

Silently I got her a glass of water; that was not so bad, since she could simply take the glass in her cupped hands and drink from it. Then she had another bite of pancake.

"I wasn't going to shoot you," she said, finally, not looking at me.

"Could have fooled me," I said. "You looked nervous enough to do just about anything."

"Yeah, well. You try bearding a mass-murderer in his den. You might have done anything."

"Whoa!" I said. "I haven't killed anybody. I was just in the wrong place at the wrong time."

"Over and over again," she said.

"Yeah, and I'm getting tired of it," I snapped. "You think I like having corpses all over the place when I'm trying to eat my lunch in peace?" Now it was my turn to scowl. "Look," I said, "Do you want some help with that?"

By this time she'd eaten the pieces of pancake I'd cut off of the stack, and was faced with the problem of cutting off more without using a knife.

"No," she said coldly, still looking down at her plate. She flipped the fork around in her hands—she really was getting quite good at it—and cut off a bit with the edge of the tines. It slowed her down a little, but not as much as you'd think.

I shrugged, and went back to the matter at hand. "So if I'm such a bad guy," I said, "why didn't *you* go to the police, huh?"

What she said next stopped me in my tracks. Well, so to speak, as I was still sitting down with my elbows on the table.

"I did," she said, looking at me at last.

"You did?" I said. My voice squeaked, and I hated myself for it. Mom was right, there were going to be more cops in my future. I swallowed a few words my mother likes to think I don't know—and then stopped. "Wait a minute...that was days ago. I haven't had any cops come to see me."

"I know."

"What do you mean, you know? Have you been watching me at home the way you've been following me around town?"

She worked another bit of pancake into her mouth, and licked the syrup off of her lips. "Can I have some coffee?" she said.

"I have no idea. I saw pancakes, I didn't see any coffee. Anyway, answer the question."

"Hmph," she said, exasperated. "I *am* answering the question. You wanted to know why I was pointing a gun at you."

I looked at her funny. "Am I missing something?"

"They wouldn't listen to me," she said. "The police. The inspector I talked to. 'You must be mistaken,' he said. 'Michael Henderson? He's harmless,' he said. He told me you were a local kid, lived here since you were born. He told me you wrote software for a living, that you paid your taxes, and that you didn't make trouble for anybody. Then he told me to change the subject."

I stared at her. "Really?" I said, astonished.

She nodded, chewing.

"He called me Michael?"

She nodded.

"Not Mikey?"

She shook her head.

"Michael."

She nodded. I couldn't believe it.

"He said that he wasn't surprised you hadn't come to the police, even if you *had* been there every time, which he didn't believe."

This did not compute. I continued to stare at her, and she just looked back at me, until I made that whirly "get on with it" motion I'd learned from my mom.

"He said that you were small for your age, and that some of the patrollers had given you a hard time before they'd figured it out. He said you had no particular reason to feel friendly about the Corey's End Police Department." She looked away. "I think he thought I was nuts anyway."

A light went on in my head. "Aha. You were the one who reported the Viking longship at Hungry Burger."

She curled her upper lip, you know how people do. "Yeah," she said.

My mind was racing. How long had it been since I'd last had a run-in with the cops? I thought back. The last time, I'd...let's see, I'd just gotten my driver's license, and I was driving Mom's car....

Ten years? Had it really been ten years?

I put that aside, and tried to focus on the matter at hand.

"Let me see if I got this. You went to the police, and told them about me, and they didn't believe you."

She nodded, chewing.

"OK. That still doesn't explain what you were doing in my living room with a gun."

"What was I supposed to do? Everywhere you went, there was blood and mayhem. People dismembered all over the place, and no one coming out alive but you." She grimaced. "And *them.* I thought you had to be helping them." She looked down. "I thought you were a scout, or a spotter, or something."

Oh. I hadn't thought about it that way.

"OK, I can see that it looked funny," I said. "But why take it so personally?"

"Somebody had to. And he could have been killed."

"He? He who?"

"Dino. Dino Balducci. He's my grandfather. He wasn't at the restaurant that day, but if he had been...."

"Dino's your grandfather?" I looked at her more closely, studying her face. Or, rather, trying to; with her head down, her face was hidden by a curtain of dampish blonde hair. I studied her hair instead. "Either you take after the other side of your family, or you dye your hair," I said finally. Of course, that would explain her eyebrows. It occurred to me to wonder why she didn't dye her eyebrows as well, and then I realized it was because she wasn't trying to hide anything. She liked being blonde, but she didn't care who knew it wasn't natural.

Her shoulders began to shake, and I realized belatedly that she was crying again.

I pulled a couple of napkins out of the stainless steel dispenser and reached them across the table to her. I had to half-stand-up to do it. "I called the Fire Department, you know," I said. "I'm glad Dino is okay. I'd wondered about that."

She took the napkins and wiped clumsily at her eyes. "Thank you," she said. "So what do we do now?"

"You asking me?"

"Nothing I've tried has been working."

"I dunno," I said. "We seem to be stuck here. Mr. Centurion seems to be a sharp kind of guy; if we could talk with him, we might get somewhere. Curiosity has to be eating him alive. I don't see how we can do it, though. His language skills are a couple of thousand years out of date."

Mystery Girl screwed up her face. It wasn't quite a smile, but it was an improvement. "I suppose I could try," she said at last. I looked at her in puzzlement.

"Catholic school," she said. "I took four years of Latin. Maybe it'll work; Church Latin is only a thousand years out of date." She shook her head. "Mr. Bertinelli'd be laughing at me if he could see me now."

She took a deep breath. "So where's your Mr. Centurion, anyway?"

Someone cleared his throat loudly, just a few feet from us, and we both jumped. Speak of the devil.

Mr. Centurion looked decidely saturnine, but his expression changed when Mystery Girl addressed him in Latin. He did one of the few real double-takes I've ever seen, and then he just stared at her, eyes wide. And then, showing that quick grasp of the situation I'd noticed before, he grabbed a chair from a nearby table and sat down. They started gabbling back and forth like— well, pretty much exactly *not* like old friends. It was like watching a tennis match between two players who were woefully out of practice. He'd serve, and she'd miss; he'd try again, and she'd look at him in perplexity; she'd try something and he'd respond; and every once in a while they actually maintained a dialog for three or four exchanges.

I put the score at about 40-30 when Mystery Girl turned to me. "How can I explain where and when he is?"

"Where, I can handle," I said. "Can you find out exactly when he's from?"

She turned back to Mr. Centurion, and I started hearing words like "Roma" and "Keezer" and "raypooblica". Meanwhile, I pulled out my smartphone and brought up Google Earth. Zooming in on Rome was a matter of moments. I adjusted it so that the whole boot of Italy was clearly visible. Then I cleared my throat.

When I had both of their attentions, I put the phone on the table, and directed Mr. Centurion's attention to the screen. I pointed at a spot about halfway up the Italian boot and said, "Roma." It was fun watching his eyes bug out. Then I played tour guide, with Mystery Girl translating the place names.

Once Mr. Centurion had grasped that we were looking at Rome and Italy, I zoomed out. I pointed out the Mediterranean Sea, and North Africa. Then I zoomed out again, and pointed out Gibraltar, France, and Great Britain. I heard Mystery Girl say, "Gallia" and "Britannia". Mr. Centurion got really excited about Britannia; I gathered that maybe he'd been there.

Then I zoomed out even farther...and spun the globe to show

North America, and pointed at our approximate location. Within, say, a state or so; it's not like precision mattered. He grunted sourly. He was an expect-the-worst kind of guy, our Mr. Centurion, and I think he was seldom disappointed.

"He recognizes Britain," said Mystery Girl. "That puts him in Julius Caesar's day, at least." Then she and he started gabbling again.

While they were occupied, I decided it was time to find out what was taking the police so long. I moved a couple of tables away, where it was a little quieter, and then spent several minutes overcoming my natural reluctance. I'd have preferred to let Mystery Girl do it, but they might ignore her; and anyway, she was busy. Finally I looked up the phone number on-line and dialed. An irritated voice answered.

"Police Department. What do you want?"

"Oh, Hi. This is Michael Henderson. Did you know that Pancake Hut has been captured by Roman soldiers?"

"Yeah, kid, tell me something I don't know."

"No, seriously, we're being held captive."

"I told you, kid, I already know about it. Look, are they killing anybody?"

I was nonplussed. "Well, no, nobody important," I said, thinking about Red Mustache lying peacefully in the shrubbery behind the restaurant.

"Count your blessings. There are swarms of little guys on ponies all over town shooting arrows at anything that moves. Trust me, you're better off where you are. Now scram."

And he hung up.

I stared at the phone for a while. How come the little guys on ponies were out there while I was in here? Not that I minded, you understand, but it didn't make sense. Of course, that begged the question of just why they'd be in with me to begin with, and that, I confess, had me stumped. And then another question occurred to me. If they were all over town, why hadn't we seen them outside the Pancake Hut?

Or why hadn't we seen them *yet*?

I went back over to Mystery Girl and Mr. Centurion, and sat down. They both looked at me, and I noticed that Mystery Girl's hands were free. The leather cords lay on the table between them.

"I think we're going to have some unwanted guests," I said.

Chapter 6

I explained about the Mongol hordes, and Mystery Girl translated, and then they gabbled back and forth for a while. Now that Mystery Girl's hands were free, she seemed to be using them just as much as her voice to get the message across.

Mr. Centurion brightened up considerably as they spoke. I gathered that making war on civilians didn't sit well with him, and that the prospect of action against a real enemy had a strong appeal. Or maybe he just didn't regard us as a real enemy, I dunno.

"He thinks they are Parthians," Mystery Girl explained when she noticed my quizzical expression. "He's seen duty in Asia, and I guess he's looking forward to having another go at them."

"There's no accounting for taste," I said. I'd been thinking while they talked, and I was about to go on when there was a clattering noise from the back of the Pancake Hut. Mr. Centurion was up and moving towards it while we were still scooting out of the booth. I trotted along after him, and Mystery Girl more or less staggered from table to table. Mr. Centurion had freed her ankles, but I guess her feet were still asleep. It would have been funny if it hadn't looked so painful. By the time we got to the far end of the restaurant her blood was flowing again and she was walking more or less normally.

A fascinating tableau awaited us. The two soldiers Mr. Centurion had left on guard were lying on the floor, with two of my fellow townsfolk sitting on each of them. The other captives, captive no longer, were frozen in the act of setting up a barricade of tables. They'd shared out the weapons; two were armed with swords, two with knives, and two others held shields. All of them had bright eyes and looked ready to snarl. Mr. Centurion was nonplussed. By this time there were several other Romans standing with him, snarling right back.

The tableau held for a long moment, until one of the Romans on the floor said something I had no trouble understanding. "Sorry, Boss," sounds about the same in every language.

Mr. Centurion just shook his head in disgust. Then he waved his men back and made a "get on with it" motion at Mystery Girl and me. I don't think he was acquainted with my mom. Anyway, the two of us stepped up to the barricade, and everybody relaxed just a trifle.

"Michael," said one of them, "what's going on?"

"There's been a misunderstanding," I said.

"Is that what you call it?" said another, I think it was Mr. McGillicuddy. That triggered a burst of general shouting and complaining. I was expecting Mr. Centurion to do something about it, but he just held back his men with one hand, and looked at me with that look of his—the one that said, "Well?" I looked back at my neighbors.

"Come on, guys," I said. "No one's been hurt, except for these two jokers here on the floor, and it looks like they'll get better quickly enough." Mystery Girl shifted as though she'd like to contest that statement; I guess her head still hurt. I ignored her. "Meanwhile, we've got the Mongol hordes roaming the streets of town. We've not seen them around here, yet, but it's only a matter of time."

"We know that," said a man I didn't know. "My wife's been texting me. But our families are out there. We need to get moving."

"Right. You're going to head home, on foot, with archers on horseback all over the place? You'd never make it."

"On foot!" exclaimed one of the fellows sitting on the right-hand guard. He was a bear of a man, dressed in a flannel shirt and a feed cap, and the guard beneath him winced as he shifted his weight. "I'd like to see them outrun my Hummer."

"No one's been hurt?" asked another as I was wondering how to explain about the barricade in the parking lot.

"Well, there was one guy killed," I said. "An old friend of ours. Remember the Viking with the red mustache? The one who skipped bail?"

"Yeah," said Mr. McGillicuddy. "So?"

"So, he's lying out back," I said. "In Roman costume." The men looked at each other, and I continued. "Look, folks. I don't think our captors really wanted to come here. I think they were brought here against their will by our late friend. Can you fault them for looking to protect themselves? They've not hurt anyone but Red Mustache, and I rather expect that Mr. Centurion here regrets his death."

Mystery Girl nodded at that, and winced.

"He does," she said. "I've been able to talk a little with him. They were preparing for battle when they showed up here, and one of his men got over-excited. After that he was just following standard procedure in a potentially hostile place. He's not sure how they got here, and he wishes that Red Mustache was here to explain it. He's got a *lot* of questions."

"So do I," I said. I rested my hands on the top of the barricade, and leaned forward. "Meanwhile, we've got Mongols. The Romans haven't hurt you, and they let the ladies go. Well, except for—" I stopped. I couldn't call her "Mystery Girl" in public, and now was no time to be asking for names. "—except for my friend here, and that's her own fault." She gave me a sharp look, but didn't contest it. "Anyway, I think we need to band together," I finished.

It occurred to me that I might want to clear this with Mr. Centurion, or least get his agreement. I turned to Mystery Girl. "Um, could you, uh..." I jerked my head at our captor. She nodded, and made with the Latin.

A few minutes later, peace and concord reigned supreme—or,

at least, a truce was tentatively established, though the guard under Brother Bear seemed disposed to argue. A stern look from Mr. Centurion quelled him, though.

Now that that was settled, it was time to start looking for answers. I turned to Mystery Girl. "Ask Mr. Centurion if we can examine Red Mustache's things," I said. She grimaced, but did as I asked. His upper lip twitched, but he grunted his assent before leading the men (both his and ours) out to prepare for battle.

As we stepped outside, there was a cry of rage and pain from the front of the Pancake Hut. Mystery Girl looked back at the door, her dark brows lowering in concern.

"It sounds like someone's hurt," she said. "The Mongols must be here. We'd better go see what we can do to help."

I waved it away. "It's not the Mongols," I said. "I think Mr. McGillicuddy just discovered what our Roman friends did to his '65 Corvette." I explained about the barricade.

Her eyes widened. "Oh. Ouch," she said, as I knelt down in the bushes by the side of the body. "Still, I really ought to be with the centurion."

"Don't be so squeamish," I said, mostly to myself, as I rummaged gingerly among Red Mustache's garments for a belt pouch or something of the sort. The light was dim, and he smelled bad, and there was that gaping hole, and I promised myself that I'd wash my hands just as soon as ever I could.

"It's not that," she said. "He needs me to translate for him."

"Yeah, maybe, but this is more important. Ah, here we go." I came up with a tooled leather pouch, just the thing that ersatz upper-class Romans wore back in the day. I cut it loose from his belt with my pocketknife, and then brought it over to the pool of light by the back door of the restaurant. The smell was bad even there, but it was better than sitting next to the corpse.

Squatting on the walkway with Mystery Girl leaning over me, I opened the pouch and laid out its contents: some shiny new Roman coins, a scrap of cloth, and a small knife in a sheath. I handed the coins to Mystery Girl, discarded the cloth, and began to give the knife a close study.

"What are we looking for, anyway?" she said.

"I thought you might be able to date our visitors from the coins.", I said. There was nothing remarkable about the sheath; it was just plain leather.

"Oh, I'm sorry, I guess I hadn't told you. Valens is from the last days of the old Roman Republic."

"Valens?"

"Gaius Valens, yes. I gather that Julius Caesar and Pompey the Great were just starting to fight over who was really going to be in charge when *he*"—she jerked her head at the body —"showed up. I think Valens was glad to be out from under, at least until he ended up here."

"Oh. Well, keep the coins anyway; you can flabbergast the folks at the museum some time." I discarded the sheath, and turned my attention to the knife itself.

It looked like a knife. A Roman knife. Or, at least, it didn't look like a modern, mass-produced knife: I wouldn't know a specifically Roman knife if it bit me. I checked the grip carefully; it was made of horn, with no decorations to hide hidden buttons, devices, or what have you. I put it down with a sigh of disgust.

"Well, that was no help."

"You still haven't answered my question," said Mystery Girl. "What are we looking for?"

I looked up at her. "Would you mind coming down here? I can't talk to you when you're towering over me like that." She grimaced, and knelt down while I settled back onto my butt and crossed my legs. I still had to look up at her, but at least I wasn't going to strain my neck. I took a deep breath.

"Red Mustache is the guy who brought the Romans and Vikings here, right?" I asked.

"Right," she said.

"We know the Vikings appeared out of nowhere and disappeared the same way, right? You saw it yourself."

"Right," she said.

"So he's traveling through time. How's he doing it?"

The corner of her mouth tightened. "Until an hour ago, I was planning on asking you that."

"Well, take a guess."

"He's a got a time machine hidden somewhere?"

"Right, except that we've seen him appear and disappear without one."

"Magic, then, I guess. It seems crazy, but what else could it be?"

"Magic or technology. I'm not ruling out magic, mind you. But it's one or the other. If it's technology, Red Mustache has to have some device to make it work, something small enough to be carried. Presumably he's got it on him. If he's just muttering magic words, we're probably out of luck. So I'm looking for the device. If we can find it, we might be able to figure out how to use it."

She frowned. "What if it's a magic device? How are you going to figure that out?"

I flashed her a grin. "No problem. Any sufficiently advanced magic is indistinguishable from software—and software is what I do."

Mystery Girl seemed unimpressed with my bravado, but she let it pass. She looked off into the distance while she considered. "If this were a novel," she said, "he'd probably have the magic ring on a chain around his neck."

"True," I said. "Care to check?"

She shuddered. She looked pretty now that she wasn't scowling at me. "Thank you, no."

Damn. Well, it had been worth a try. I scrambled up and stepped back into the bushes. After a few moments—as few as I could reasonably contrive—I said, "Well, it looks like you were right." I held up a round leather object about two inches long by about three-quarters of an inch thick. It was suspended on a thin leather strap. "Let's see what it is."

I brought it back to where Mystery Girl knelt in the pool of light, and sat down. I turned the thing over in my hands. "Yup, this is it," I said. "See here? It's a case, and it snaps closed. No Roman made this."

"So open it already," she said, leaning in toward me. I kind of liked that. When you're small for your age, the girls don't pay much attention to you...or if they do, you usually wish they hadn't. Mystery Girl was different. Granted, she'd almost shot me, but I thought maybe I could overlook that.

The case snapped open at one end, and inside was a snuggly fitting cylinder of dark metal with thin, spidery markings all over it. I couldn't tell whether it was writing, or just decoration. It had a worn, silvery disc embedded on one end—the end that was visible when the case was first opened. The other end was smooth and rounded.

"Lipstick?" I said.

Mystery Girl gave me a look. I looked back, and shrugged. "I don't see any controls on this, except for this silver disk," I said. "Care to give it a press?"

She pursed her lips, and frowned. "I'm not sure that that's a good idea. Who knows what might happen?"

"It's a lousy idea. But I don't see a User's Guide floating around anywhere, do you? How else are we going to find out what it does? Anyway, I don't see any kind of controls here. I'm betting that pushing the button turns the thing on, and opens up some kind of control mechanism."

"I guess that makes sense. Tell you what, you hold it, and I'll press the button. If this thing sends me to ancient Egypt, I don't want to go by myself."

"Works for me," I said, holding it out.

Mystery Girl took my hand in both of hers, and positioned her right thumb over the silver disc. "Ready?" she asked.

No, I thought to myself. I wasn't at all ready. In fact, I rather wanted to execute Plan A. But I couldn't tell her that. So I said "Quit stalling," instead.

She took a deep breath, and pressed her thumb firmly down on the disc.

There was a long moment in which absolutely nothing

happened, except that I was very aware of her hands on mine.

After that, nothing continued to happen.

Finally, Mystery Girl smiled brightly. "Well, that didn't work," she said, and took her hands away.

"Hmph," I grunted. "There's got to be some way to make it work." I turned it over and over in my hands, looking at it from different directions and trying to make sense of the markings. They *almost* seemed to make sense, once in a while, and then they were just odd wavy lines again.

After a couple of minutes, Mystery Girl touched me on the arm.

"Do you hear that?"

I lowered the device, and cocked an ear.

Hoof beats. Lots of them.

I put the Thingy back in its case and slung the strap around my neck.

"We'd better take this inside," I said.

Beating a hasty retreat into the Pancake Hut might not seem particularly heroic; all I can say in my defense is that I have a rather unheroic build. When you're small for your age, you learn that meeting force with force is rarely a profitable endeavor. As for Mystery Girl, her pistol was still safely ensconced in my apartment.

Not that it mattered. I gave Mystery Girl better than average odds that she'd pull the trigger in the face of imminent Mongol attack; I was rather less confident about her ability to hit what she shot at...or to cope with the results.

Then I remembered her determination with the pancakes. She'd cope with the results, all right; but I didn't want to be one of them.

So inside we went; and of course we went back to the table near the cash register, where we could peer through the window and try to see what was going on in the darkness in front of the restaurant.

It was rather an anti-climax.

What we had here was a classic case of mismatched forces. The Romans were well forted up behind their barricade, but their only ranged weapons were a pair of wicked looking javelins carried by each man—very effective as two forces on foot come together, but not much use against cavalry. And anyway, the javelins had been distributed to Mr. McGillicuddy and company, who otherwise would have been unarmed, and so of not much use as defenders.

For their part, the Mongols were mobile, and armed with bows and arrows, but cavalry isn't much good against a fortified position. The best they could do was stand off out of javelin range, and race around in circles, and whoop and holler, and send the occasional arrow over the barricade. We could hear them much better than we could see them; the Mongols were short, and their ponies were short, so even in daylight not much would have shown over the wall. A few of them were carrying torches, and we saw these as points of fire going back and forth in the dimness of the street lights.

In short, we couldn't get at them, and they couldn't get at us without getting off of their ponies—and let me tell you, a man who thinks that riding a pony into Lee's #1 Grocery Store is a *good* idea isn't likely to dismount for a mingy century of Roman soldiers forted up in the Pancake Hut.

I think the only one of our guys who was hurt while I was watching was Mr. McGillicuddy, who winced visibly every time an arrow hit his beloved Corvette. And every time it happened, Brother Bear reached out a massive paw and patted Mr. McGillicuddy sympathetically on the shoulder; and every time an arrow hit Brother Bear's Hummer, he put his head back and laughed. He was not only useful, he had a good attitude, our Brother Bear.

Eventually the torches winked out and the whooping and hollering faded, to be replaced by the glow of camp fires as the Mongols settled down for the night.

There was one incident of note. The one weak point in the barricade was, paradoxically, its strongest point, to wit, the

Hummer. It was too big to smash through, but as I'd noted earlier a person of reasonable size could wriggle underneath...and the Mongols were much more reasonably sized than most people I know. I blame nutrition.

Anyway, Brother Bear and Mr. McGillicuddy had taken up stations in Brother Bear's Hummer, where they were simultaneously protected from attack and could keep an eye on the Mongols outside. Brother Bear had turned off the lights in the cab, and the windows were tinted in any event, so I don't think the Mongols knew they were there. I could see them only because the doors on the restaurant side of the Hummer were hanging open.

Consequently, Brother B and Mr. M were on the spot when, a little after midnight, one intrepid Mongol tried to wriggle through and take us by surprise. I missed it, of course, being heartily bored with the whole thing by that time, and tired of pressing my face up against the window. But Brother B was keeping careful watch, and when the infiltrator squirmed out from under the Hummer, Brother B came down on him like a ton of bricks. He didn't need to use his javelin; he just dropped down, feet first, on the small of the Mongol's back.

Have I mentioned that Brother Bear wears steel-toed work boots? It's a wonder he didn't break the man's back. But he certainly knocked all of the wind out of him, and our Roman allies had him trussed up like a Thanksgiving turkey in minutes.

Shortly thereafter, Brother Bear and Mr. Centurion came in for a confab with Mystery Girl, after which Brother B cheerfully used his javelin to puncture the sidewalls of all four of his Hummer's tires. (I don't like to think about what he had to do to get to the outer pair.) The big SUV settled to the ground. The gap underneath was still sizable, but at least it was less inviting than it had been.

See, this is what I mean by a good attitude. Brother Bear doesn't sweat the small stuff, and next to him it's *all* small stuff. He's a good guy for a giant.

* * *

Meanwhile, I'd been alternating between fiddling with the Thingy, taking quick looks out the window, and dozing. I'd even tried doing a web search, and as I can tell you from personal experience, Googling "Thingy with strange markings" is Not Helpful. That was a desperation move, and afterwards I kind of drifted off. I was nearly sound asleep when Brother Bear and Mr. Centurion came in to take advantage of Mystery Girl Translation Services, Inc. They didn't stay long but it woke me up pretty thoroughly, so I took the Thingy out of its case again.

It looked just like it had the previous fifty times I'd studied it. Dark metal, check. Markings that might be writing, check. Markings that might not be writing, check. Inert silver disk, check. Bloody infuriating lack of response, check. I use the word "infuriating" precisely, because the thing really was making me angry. I was beginning to feel like it was laughing at me. All I wanted was for it to *do* something, to repay my attention in some way. I wanted the darn thing to do what I told it to do. In frustration, I wrenched at it with both hands, trying for the twenty-seventh time to see if it could be opened, or if there were moving parts I couldn't detect. I dunno, maybe I thought it needed a new set of AA batteries. Maybe I was just venting my anger.

And the thingy *moved*. I could feel the markings shifting under my fingers, taking on new shapes. I gasped, and nearly dropped it on the table.

However it was that I had done it, the thingy had quite clearly turned itself on. The body of it remained dark, but the markings were glowing like burning blue threads. It looked like something out of a video game.

Mystery Girl started when I gasped, and leaned across the table to get a closer look.

"You did it!" she said, putting her hand on my wrist. Her dark brows furrowed. "What did you do?"

"I have no idea," I said. "I was angry with it, and gave it a yank, and then this happened."

"Better be careful, then. Who knows what you might do by

mistake?"

I was about to agree, but it was at that moment that the Mongols attacked in force.

We'd had a weak point none of us had considered: those Mongol ponies could *jump*. Not too high, and not too far, but high enough to reach the hood of, say, a 1965 Corvette, and then down the other side. Even good Detroit steel can't take that kind of punishment forever, but by the time it crumpled the damage was done, and twenty or so Mongols had made it inside the barricade. Mr. Centurion had let half the men stand down and get some sleep, and while those remaining were watchful none of them had expected an out-and-out frontal assault at that hour.

Frankly, I don't think anyone has given proper attention to the effect of modern street lights on ancient methods of warfare. I know I hadn't. And other than noting the fact, I had no time in the middle of an attack to ponder it in detail.

I could hear Mr. Centurion encouraging his men to have at them, and various shouts and curses from the rank and file and guttural shrieks from the Mongols. They were out for our blood, and didn't care who knew it. I thought the Romans would prevail, but I hadn't survived twenty-six years in the Land of the Giants by hanging around when a fight broke out. There was nowhere to run, but I had to get away.

Mystery Girl's hand was still resting lightly on my wrist. I put my left hand over it, it holding it tight, and pushed the silver disc with my right thumb. The glowing blue markings shifted. And everything turned inside out and changed color.

Chapter 7

Mystery Girl was furious with me.

"How could you go and leave them like that?" She was braiding her long hair into a ponytail. She'd often done it before, clearly, because she wasn't at all paying attention to what she was doing. Instead, she was casting her evil eye on me from under stormy brows. Thunder and lightning were distinct possibilities, and given the fire in her eyes, so was sunburn.

Not real sunburn, of course. Dehydration, possibly, or maybe a good roasting, but not sunburn; the canvas roof over our head protected us from that. It was hot inside, though, and I was sweating freely.

We were sitting in a kind of tent, or tent cabin. It wasn't very large, perhaps eight feet square, with a wooden floor and canvas walls and roof. There was one cot and one stool, and a pile of stuff in one corner. Mystery Girl had the stool, which she occupied in a posture of pointed indignation. Pointed, that is, at me, where I was sprawled on the cot.

I should have let Mystery Girl take the cot, but I confess the thought didn't even occur to me at the time, I was that tired.

Outside, the sun beat down on a dry, reddish landscape of rocks, gravel, and dust. It looked a lot like pictures I'd seen of the surface of Mars, only less inviting, and not as flat. A massive butte rose behind the tent cabin, and other buttes and pillars of red stone were dimly visible on the horizon through the dust hanging in the air. I suppose it could have been majestic, but I was too hot and tired to care.

We'd found ourselves in front of the tent after a timeless moment of exceeding weirdness that I can't possibly describe. There was nothing else of interest as far as we could see for the dust, and with the red sun scorching us through a reddish overcast we'd lost little time in investigating the tent. Once inside, the burning sun had quickly been replaced by the burning scowl.

"What did you expect me to do, hang around and get killed?" I retorted. "I didn't get to be this age by not running from danger. That's Plan A."

She flushed. "You didn't run when I came to your apartment. I've still got bruises on my shins." She finished her braid with a rubber band, wrapping it tightly around with sharp forceful motions of her fingers. I was glad it wasn't my neck.

"You were between me and the door," I retorted, stung.

"So you only knock people down when you're cornered?"

"Well, yeah. Look, it's simple. Plan A is to get out of Dodge. If you can't run, then you try Plan B: you hide, and hope they don't see you. If you can't hide, *then* you use Plan C. And you go back to Plan A as soon as you can."

She sniffed. "And then, after you knocked me down, you jumped on my back," she said, crossing her arms. "What plan was that?"

She had me there.

"Look, nobody's perfect. Next time, I promise I'll keep going." I yawned. "Anyway," I said through the yawn, trying to sound like the voice of sweet reason, "what good could we have done if we'd stayed?"

"We could have helped with the wounded. You could have run messages, or carried water like you were doing earlier. And Valens needs me to translate. If they all get killed, it might be your fault."

I chuckled sourly. "Translation's not going to be a problem. Turns out that Valens speaks English as well as you or I do."

Mystery Girl flipped her pony-tail back over her shoulder, and looked at me funny.   Angry and funny, an interesting combination. "What on earth are you talking about?"

I leaned back on the cot.   "Just before we left, I heard him shouting orders at the troops. In English."

Now she looked worried.   "Michael, he was shouting in Latin."

"It was English, damn it! I heard him plain as day. He was telling his men to lock shields and form a defensive line."

"That might be what he said. I couldn't make it out, he was talking too fast. But he certainly wasn't saying it in English." She leaned forward, studying my face.   "Michael, are you feeling OK? You look pale."

"I'm feeling fine," I shouted. "Look, Myster-" I broke off. I could hardly call her that to her face.

Her eyes narrowed. "'Look, Mister'? You've been watching too many Star Trek re-runs."

I waved a hand, as though erasing what I'd just said. "What *is* your name, anyway?"

"Bernie. Bernie Balducci. I thought you'd never ask." She was glaring at me again, and her glare was nicely complemented by the waves of heat coming through the canvas of the tent.

"So I'm socially retarded. I live with my mother, remember?" I snorted. "Bernie? Really? It fits," I said. "Are you sure you aren't really a red head?"

"What's that supposed to mean?"

"Never mind. Why 'Bernie'?"

"St. Bernadette, of course."

"Oh." I shrugged. "Bernie. Okay, I'll remember that."

Mystery Girl—no, Bernie—slumped on her stool.

"So when are we, anyway?" She waved her hand at the arid landscape on the other side of the canvas. "And where? This certainly doesn't look like the land around Corey's End."

"In the middle of nowhere, is all I know.   Some desert somewhere. You saw it." I yawned again. "Could be Australia, could be Arizona. I dunno when we are, either.   Could be 5 million years B.C."

"B.C.? What about this tent?"

"The tent looks like a bolt-hole. I can't imagine Red Mustache spent much time here, but it makes sense that he'd have a safe place to escape to."

"That explains that, then," she said, looking at the floor below me.

"Explains what?"

"That, under the cot."

I rolled painfully over onto my stomach—all my muscles were sore—and peeked under the cot. There was a set of black motorcycle leathers I'd last seen in the parking lot of Johansen's Department Store. "Ah. Those. Yes, yes it does." I rolled over again, and closed my eyes.

A few moments later, Bernie rolled her eyes—trust me on this, it was audible—and I heard her moving about. When I looked up, she was on her knees rummaging through the pile of stuff in the corner. I watched without much interest.

"Finding anything?" I asked after a couple of minutes. Getting up to go look for myself was just too much effort.

"I think this box might contain field rations," she said. "It's filled with boxes sealed in black plastic." She turned to the next. "Aha! Water!" She pulled out a clear bottle with a label on it. She frowned at it. "At least, I think it must be water. I can't make heads or tails of this label."

I sat up as she handed it to me. My legs felt like they were made of lead.

"It seems perfectly plain to me," I said. "Mountain spring water, it says, from the slopes of Mount Denalish. Denalish Bottling Company, Denalish, Calahosis. One Zwieback." That didn't sound right, but I was too tired to pursue it.

"One...zwieback?"

"That's what it says. I don't know whether that's the price or the volume, though." I twisted off the metal cap, and sniffed at it.

Bernie pulled out another bottle, and studied the label.

"Michael," she said, softly, still looking at the label.

"Yeah?" I took a cautious sip. It tasted like water.

"When did you first hear Gaius Valens speaking English?"

"I told you. Right when the Mongols came over the barricade."

"Right after you woke that thing up, you mean."

"Yeah, I guess....so. Oh." I looked down at the leather case resting on my chest. I'd put the Thingy back into it for safe keeping when we entered the tent. "So Valens *wasn't* speaking English."

Blessedly, Bernie refrained from saying, "I told you so." I don't know how she managed it.

"Here, take a look at this," she said. She passed me one of the black plastic packages. I took it in my left hand, careful not to spill the water.

There was a label in one corner. "Calahosis Ready Meal. Turkey tetrazini, pepper crackers, processed animal preserves, merchant oil. Feeds one. Calahosis Camping Supply."

"'Merchant oil'? 'Processed animal preserves'?"

I shrugged. "At least we won't starve. Assuming we stay here for any length of time." I took another drink and passed Bernie the bottle of water.

"I don't see why we should," she said.

"Anything else over there?" I asked. I was still sleepy, but my stomach rumbled, loudly enough to make Bernie jump.

"No. Just more of the same."

A thought occurred to me. I put the meal down and pulled the Thingy out of its case. If I could read the labels, maybe I could make sense of...but no. The markings were still glowing, but they were still as inscrutable as ever. I sighed, and put it away again.

Bernie had opened one of the packages as I looked at the Thingy, and began nibbling on one of the pepper crackers. She made a face.

"Any good?"

"Not so you'd notice."

My stomach rumbled again, and hunger came over me in a wave. "Pass it over here," I said. "Quick."

The crackers *did* taste a little odd, at first, but on the whole they were OK. The processed animal preserves were in a little plastic tub with a foil top. There was something like a short popsicle stick in the box, and I used it to spread some of the preserves on the crackers. That tasted odd, too, pepper and salt and vinegar and other flavors I couldn't name. I didn't like it, exactly, but I couldn't seem to stop eating. The turkey tetrazini was in a larger plastic tub. When I peeled back the foil it looked like nothing I'd ever seen before, and it was dehydrated besides, but I didn't let that stop me. I just poured in some water, stirred it a bit, and shoveled it down with the help of the popsicle stick.

The merchant oil was in a little plastic packet, like ketchup. I left it alone, although I did wonder idly how many merchants you needed to squeeze to make one packet of oil.

Pangs of hunger stilled, fatigue rolled back in. I think Bernie was saying something, but I was too tired to pay attention. I curled up on the cot, and I was out.

When I woke up, there was a whole lot of shaking going on. Bernie was shaking me, to begin with, and calling my name; she seemed exercised about something. The ground was shaking, too, and as I crawled back to consciousness I could hear noises that seemed to go with the shaking.

First, there was a low-pitched but rapid galumphing noise: *ga-LUMPH, ga-LUMPH, ga-LUMPH, ga-LUMPH, ga-LUMPH!* Behind that there was a deeper, slower thumping: *THUD. THUD. THUD.* Both noises seemed to be getting closer, and I began to understand why Bernie was exercised.

I climbed to my feet, muscles still aching. I know that's not all that far to climb, but it sure seemed like a long way. Bernie took me by the hand, and pulled me stumbling to the door of the tent, which was open. The sounds were getting louder, and the floor shook more and more strongly with each progressive *ga-LUMPH!*

We stepped out, and Bernie pointed to the right.

"Over there, look!"

I looked.

There was a cloud of reddish dust billowing up in the distance, like the cloud that rises up behind a car on a dirt road. And at the head of the cloud, where the car would be, was a *thing*. A large, snarling thing. An enormous, four-legged snarling thing with teeth and a long red tongue. It was covered with fur that might have been white under the dust, and when I say it was enormous, I mean it was as big as a house. Not a little shack, but the kind of old family home that's grown over the generations, throwing out wings here and there like an amoeba—the sort of house that if it had been in a movie, it would have its own theme music. But I couldn't hear any music. Instead, all I could hear was the sound the thing's paws made when they hit the ground.

Ga-LUMPH, ga-LUMPH, ga-LUMPH!

I gripped Bernie's hand tightly, and she gripped back, and as the thing raced closer I realized that the flatness and emptiness of the plain had caused me to misjudge its size. It was much farther away than I'd realized—and thank God for that—but it wasn't as big as a house. It was far bigger, and the reddish-pink cloud of dust towered up into the air behind it.

Ga-LUMPH, ga-LUMPH, ga-LUMPH!

And behind that, lost in the cloud of dust, *THUD. THUD. THUD.* Over the din I heard Bernie saying, "It's time to go, Michael! Use that thing! It's time to go!"

The beast was still miles away, and already it towered over us, snarling and snapping. The nostrils in its damp black nose looked large enough to drive a city bus into. I let go of Bernie, and with shaking hands I pulled the leather case around in front of me and unsnapped the cover.

I looked at Bernie, and made to take her hand again, and then her eyebrows shot up and her eyes widened. She held up her index finger, and dashed inside. I looked from her to the beast and back again, almost dancing in terror, but in seconds she was back, clutching a bottle of water and two of the ready meals. She tucked the bottle under one arm, took a firm hold of my left hand, and nodded.

The clouds of dust parted behind the beast, just for a moment, and as I pushed the silver disc with all my might we saw, looming high above its shaggy back, the dirty red knees of its master.

There was a timeless interval of exceeding weirdness that I can't possibly describe, and then we were leaning on a wall of gray stone.

"Bernie," I said, panting, my heart pounding a mile a minute.

"Yeah?" she said. Her hand began to relax, but I held on tightly.

"I'll never think of you as a giant again. I promise."

Chapter 8

We walked in shadow on sand-strewn paths between high gray walls. We walked side by side and hand in hand. And if anything yet lived in this cold, gray place we didn't particularly want to meet it. I clutched the Thingy in its case with my free hand, its lid already unsnapped—or, rather, still unsnapped.

Neither of us spoke. We walked because the thought of lingering in the narrow way between the gray walls was intolerable. We walked in shadow along the paths because the darkness we saw through the doorless openings on either side was unspeakable. To our right and left, darkness; beneath our feet, the sound of sand gritty on stone; so far above our heads, the narrow river of sky. The sky was a deep blue—not the blue of night, but not the blue of honest day either. It was not a comfort to us.

Neither of us wanted to be there. We stayed only because we were afraid to end up someplace worse.

There was no movement but our own. No clouds moving across the sky; no signs of life; no breath of wind.

Frankly, it was depressing as all get out.

The paths were five to six feet wide. The walls on either hand were constructed of tightly fitting blocks of stone, flat on their faces but varying wildly in shape—not a natural irregularity, as though the builders had used whatever boulders came to hand, but an angular, hard-edged irregularity of straight lines and rectilinear extrusions, suggesting monstrous forms with arms and tentacles of stone spinning out and clasping each other in eternal embrace—or combat.

The individual stones were immense, and I had an unpleasant suspicion that they might be cyclopean. At least the angles were all familiar. At the first sight of strange non-Euclidean angles I was pushing that button, come what may.

Fantastic structures of wrought metal punctuated the way, climbing up walls to narrow windows high above our heads, and standing in the center of the occasional intersections. Branches and sprays of metal extended from them to buildings on either hand. The metal arms and branches and buttresses were perforated throughout with holes of all shapes and sizes: circles, stars, shapes with no name. Though crusted with a purplish-blue verdigris, the metal appeared perfectly solid to my casual glance.

We had walked for some while, and I was beginning to feel hungry—ravenous, in fact—when Bernie stopped and I perforce stopped with her. She might not be a giant, but she still outweighs me by considerable. She was looking quizzically at a spot on the wall of the gigantic building on our left.

"Michael," she said, "What's that up there?"

"It's all 'up there'," I said, which earned me a Look.

The walls we'd seen so far had been uniformly flat, except for the grooves where the weirdly shaped blocks of stone met in their eternal embrace. Here, though, a rectangular patch was inset an inch or two into the stone. The patch was about fifteen inches wide and ten high, and its lower edge was about eight feet from the ground. It was hard to see it clearly in the shadows, not to mention at that height, but it seemed that the stone within the inset was anything but smooth. In fact....

One of the metal structures climbed the wall to my right and swayed one branch over the path to brush the wall on the other side. At one point it passed within a couple of feet of the rectangular patch. I closed the Thingy's case, making sure it was snapped firmly shut, and dropping Bernie's hand I approached the wrought metal and started to climb, the purple corrosion rough under my fingers. I'm good at climbing; it's a survival skill.

It wasn't a pleasant task, as many of the holes were too small for my hands and feet, and so I had to cling with my fingers and put my feet in openings that pinched them cruelly. Many of the larger holes seemed to have serrated edges, too dull to cut, but too sharp to bear my weight without pain. Fortunately I don't weigh that much. Eventually I was hanging from a cross-piece high over Bernie's head, with my own head a foot or so from the wall. The cross piece was studded with sharp diamond-shapes, and I wasn't sure how long I'd be able to hang on.

As to getting down, I thought that might not be a problem.

It was hard, but I managed to turn my attention to the matter at hand. As I had thought, there were marks engraved on the inset patch of wall. Writing of some kind, perhaps; if so, I couldn't read it. But I didn't need to read it to recognize the style of it, or to pull out the Thingy to do a detailed comparison. I stared at the engraving, just as I had at the ones on the thingy, trying to make them make sense. They didn't. Finally, my hands and legs aching, I removed my left hand from the serrated hole where it was wedged, and reached out and began to trace the engravings with my fingers.

And then I said, "Ow!" and whipped my fingers back, and jerked like you do when there's a loud noise as you're just falling asleep, and that was too much for my right arm, which slipped, except that my right foot was caught and so I fell head first, almost in slow motion, to the sand-strewn pavement so many feet below.

Bernie gasped and tried to catch me, but she'd backed away to watch what I was doing, and she was a little too slow. Instead, we went down together in a painful tangle. The drifted sand was deeper than usual just there or I might have broken my head. As it was, I thought I'd have an awfully sore neck in the morning.

Just for the record, I am not in the habit of sweeping young ladies off of their feet—nor they, me—and yet, it looked like becoming a regular occurrence with Bernie. Hmmm. I filed that thought away for future reference.

"What happened?" she asked when we'd sorted ourselves out. "Why did you jump like that?"

"I dunno," I said. "It felt like it *bit* me." I held up my left hand, and we studied my finger tips. I frowned. There was no blood, no scrapes, nothing to account for the bright stab of pain I'd felt, nothing to show that I hadn't imagined it. Had I imagined it, that brief flash of blue from the groove my fingers had been tracing? I didn't think so. All the hairs on my arms and legs stood up, and I shivered.

We picked ourselves up and brushed the sand off of our clothes, and in my case out of my hair. No comb, curse the luck. I'd lost my comb days before, probably while dodging Vikings. I unsnapped the cover of the Thingy's case, and took Bernie's hand, and we continued walking.

Some time later, my stomach rumbled so loudly that it seemed to echo, at least internally. "I'm going to need to eat, soon," I said. "Something about using the Thingy really seems to take it out of me." I could feel Bernie's shudder through her hand. Apparently she wasn't reconciled to processed meat preserves and merchant oil.

"OK," she said, "But not here. I just...I don't want to stop here in the dark, with all of these doors. Let's see if we can find someplace more open."

So we kept walking down one path and then other, always turning our faces toward the light wherever the paths met. After perhaps twenty minutes we came to an intersection where a path struck off diagonally to our right. This was new, as the other crossings we'd seen had all met more or less at right angles. The intersection was larger than most, too, and the metal spire at its center taller and more ornate. There seemed to be fewer shadows down the diagonal path, and it was wider, and so thither we went.

The light grew as we walked, and for the first time we began to hear a sound other than the sound of our own footsteps on sandy pavement, the first sound we hadn't caused ourselves: a dull hum, a distant rumble, like the sound of a busy highway across the valley in the small hours of the night. We looked at each other with no small amount of apprehension, but we kept walking. And as we walked, the sound grew louder.

At length we emerged into a wan light and the largest space we'd yet seen. It was a broad square perhaps a quarter-mile on a side, filled with drifted sand and devoid of buildings and metal branch-work. And at last we saw the sun, a bright hard point of blue that gave no warmth, but only that prickly sensation that makes you reach for your sunscreen. No comb, and no sunscreen. Obviously, I was never a boy scout.

The scene was almost unbearably bleak, in that empty, sand-filled square, with the massive gray buildings rising uninvitingly on all sides, black windows staring, blocks of stone locked in eternal combat with each other, metal climbing the walls like dead vines.

The center of the square was separated from the buildings by thirty or forty yards of sand, patches of pavement showing through here and there; beyond that was a low wall, maybe three or so feet high, that blocked our view of the ground beyond. The wall ran off in both directions, and I guessed that it surrounded the entire interior of the square. From where we were standing, I couldn't see any gates or openings in the wall.

The sound was louder, and seemed to be rising from the middle of the square, not that we could see anything.

"Let's go over there," said Bernie. "If we have to sit on the ground, I'd rather sit with my back to that wall and keep an eye on the buildings. I don't *think* anything's going to come out of them, but still..."

I nodded. It might seem silly, but I felt the same way: something about the city was not to be trusted.

"That wall reminds a little of the wall around Corey Park," I said. "If this was a park, maybe there will be places to sit on the other side of the wall."

"*Nothing* about this place reminds me in the least of Corey Park," said Bernie. "I'd much rather be there than here."

Still, we trudged on. The sand was deeper, here, and I could feel it getting inside my shoes. Joy.

The sound grew louder yet as we approached the wall, and got our first look at what was really on the other side. The wall was taller than I'd realized, and I had to stand on tip-toe to look over, wincing as I craned my neck. Yes, I'd be sore in the morning. Bernie, of course, had no trouble.

It wasn't a park, and there was no place to sit.

The wall wasn't simply a wall at all, but a parapet, for on the other side it dropped straight down into a chasm. The sides of the chasm were bound with the same blocks of writhing gray stone and black gaping windows as we'd seen throughout the city. Fantastic sprays of wrought metal climbed along them and leaped from one side to the other. We could not see the bottom.

Directly across from us was the source of the strange noise we'd been hearing, a noise which suddenly sounded all too familiar. On the far side of the chasm, perhaps fifty yards down from the edge, was a gaping black gash running horizontally along the face, as though a giant had punched his fist through the stone over and over again. We could make out the remains of window openings and dangling metal around its edges. And from all along its length poured a vast cataract of water, spilling endlessly down into the depths and filling that side of the chasm with mist. As the water cascaded through the branches and arms of metal, it added a harsh, thrumming undertone to the sound of the torrent.

We stood there and watched it for a long time. There was an updraft from the chasm, maybe due to all that falling water, and wisps of Bernie's hair blew this way and that.

"I had been thinking that this place was dead, that it was a corpse," said Bernie, when we had sat down, backs to the wall. "Then we heard the sound of the waterfall, and I began to think I was mistaken." She shook her head. "Now I see that it isn't even a corpse. There's nothing alive about this place, not even weeds, not even moss on the wall over there. It's just bones."

"Maybe," I said, tearing at the black wrapper of the meal

she'd handed me. "It's still creepy, though." I was more than ravenous, now; hunger consumed me, and I was beginning to feel that if it took only a few more bites there'd be nothing left. I was so hungry that I even opened the squeeze packet of merchant oil, which proved to be a substance mostly but not entirely unlike melted peanut butter. I ate it on the pepper crackers with the processed meat preserves, and washed down the dehydrated tetrazini with water from Mt. Denalish. Bernie had some water, and then watched me eat with distaste.

When I was done, I wondered what to do with the trash. I thought about throwing it over the wall into the chasm, but that seemed tacky, and anyway I didn't want Bernie to furrow her brows at me. In the end I stuffed the remains into my pockets...and found some change. Littering was wrong, but throwing pennies into fountains, well, that was a tradition. I stood up, and peering over the wall I tossed the penny as far as I could. We watched it disappear into the mist.

"Got another?" Bernie asked. I dug out a second penny, and handed it to her, and she sent it after its fellow with a deft sideways toss, like she was skipping stones. It sailed out farther than mine, and rebounded from an arm of purple metal before vanishing into the depths. The sound of the collision was lost in the roar of the water.

"Well, we can't stay here forever," I was saying, because I was tired of standing on tip-toe, when from across the way, down one of paths off to our right, came a high-pitched tapping sound, as of someone banging gently on a piece of metal with a hammer.

Following the tapping noise was undoubtedly foolish, but I think we were both so hungry for some sign of life that we couldn't resist. We didn't discuss it; we just turned away from the brink of the abyss and headed toward the source of the sound. Our curiosity is probably the only thing that saved us.

Whatever was tapping was farther away than it seemed; sound carried in that cold, unpleasant atmosphere. The tapping was intermittent, and there were intervals during which we wondered whether it would ever start up again.

"At least we don't need to worry about getting lost," I said quietly. "Around here, one place is as bad as another."

"Silly me," said Bernie. "And here I thought we were already lost."

That shut me up.

We kept walking, following the sound as it started and stopped.

After one long silence the tapping resumed, louder than ever, and seemingly almost at my elbow. We turned a corner, and started in surprise. The tapping sound *was* made by someone banging gently on a piece of metal with a hammer.

The someone in question was a short, fat fellow in a pith helmet and khakis. Well, I say "short." He was rather taller than me, but shorter than Bernie. He had a rock hammer in one hand, and was tapping gently on a section of metal that was twining up the wall in front of him. I have no idea what he was trying to accomplish. He looked so much like an explorer from an old movie that I began to wonder where his native bearers were. Then I began to wonder what they might look like, which was probably a mistake.

He was facing away from us as we turned the corner, but I guess we made some noise when we saw him, because *he* jumped too. When he turned to look at us we saw that he wore round spectacles, and had the kind of bushy eyebrows that make small children hide behind their mothers. His eyes widened behind the spectacles, and as I groped for words he cocked his head to one side in an attitude of listening. His eyes grew even wider. He slid the hammer into a loop on his belt with practiced ease, reached inside his jacket, and vanished.

Bernie and I looked at each other.

"I showered this morning," I said.

"That was yesterday," she said, and then for the first time I noticed that although the deep roar of the waterfall was all but lost in the distance, the harsh, thrumming tone I'd noticed while watching it seemed to have followed us.

In fact, in seemed to be getting louder.

In fact, not only was it getting louder, it was clearly getting closer as well. From the echoes, it was only a few turns behind us. I looked at Bernie.

"Plan A?" she asked. I nodded, and I reached for the Thingy as we both started to run for our lives.

Chapter 9

When I came to myself, a seeming eternity later, I was lying on the floor with my face ground into the deep pile carpet. The whole front of my body ached, and my right cheek burned. I could hear a radio playing somewhere afar off, some talking head saying something about Mongols. Bernie's hand, rough with grit, still clutched mine. My heart was pounding like mad.

The radio switched off, and a voice said, "Michael, you seem to be making a habit of sweeping this young lady off of her feet. Don't you think you ought to introduce me?"

Something familiar about that idea. "I'll think about it," I said indistinctly. My eyes remained closed, and I thought I better hadn't ought to move from my spot on the deep pile carpet.

There was something familiar about the feel of the carpet, too. "Michael."

Something familiar about that voice. It was the voice that told me things like, "Michael, get over yourself." Although, it seemed to me that there was a hint more concern in it than I was used to hearing. I waited to see if I'd hear the arms cross or the foot tap.

Instead, the voice came again, "Michael?"

Yes, there was definitely a note of concern. How nice—maybe I wasn't in trouble after all. I turned my head just a little, wincing, so that my mouth wasn't buried in the deep pile, and maybe the voice could hear me.

"Hi, Mom," I said. "Mom, this is Bernie Balducci. Bernie,

this is Mom."

"Pleased to meet you," Bernie said. Her voice was muffled, and she didn't move, either.

A long moment passed, and I used it to continue to renew my acquaintance with the carpet. It smelled dusty. Funny how even the cleanest carpet still smells dusty. My heart rate was beginning to slow, which was nice. Adrenaline is a useful tool, but I'd hate to have to live with it all the time.

"Well," said the voice. "I suppose I'd best get dinner on the table. Your father was always ravenous when he came back from one of his trips. He usually came back more quietly, though."

Ravenous? I thought. Ravenous, yes, that too. Aching muscles, check, pounding heart, check, shooting pains in my neck and shoulder, check, rug-burned cheek, check, left hand starting to go to sleep, check, ravenous appetite. Check. Oh, and sand in my socks. I hate that.

"Dinner," I said to the carpet. "Yeah, that'd be great."

Wait a minute. My father? Mom *never* talked about my father. I tried to raise my head, but it didn't want to go. It didn't matter, though, as Mom had left the room. I could hear her footsteps on the kitchen tiles.

Bernie's hand relaxed slowly, and pulled gently away. I was sorry for it to go. I hadn't often held hands with a girl, and I thought maybe I rather liked it, even with the sand and grit. But she let go and climbed slowly to her feet. I stayed where I was as Bernie limped off after Mom.

Time passed, and more aches began to distinguish themselves in my mind. There was one spot in particular, on the right-hand side of my ribcage, where there was a hard knot of pain. I thought about it for a while. Eventually I concluded that it was the Thingy, and that I was lying on it. I'd have to do something about that. I winced again.

The Thingy. I'd finally managed to press the button on that darn Thingy. When I'd sat down to eat my meal by the chasm, I'd snapped closed the cover on the Thingy's case, and swung it around to hang behind me, out of the way. Somehow I hadn't gotten it ready to hand when we started to follow the tapping of the hammer. When whatever it was started to chase us—and to this day I don't know precisely what it was, and I am content to remain in ignorance—which is to say, I am content to remain in one piece—I was completely unprepared. So I grabbed Bernie's hand, and we ran. We ran as fast as we could, pushing off of the walls and swinging around the corners on outcroppings of metal, and slipping on the sand half of the time, while I tried to pull the case around in front of me with my free hand. It was hung cross-wise over my left shoulder, so when I pulled the strap, the case climbed further up my back instead of coming around in front where I wanted it.

The sound was getting louder, a harsh buzzing and thrumming. I began to picture giant locusts. Giant hairy man-eating locusts with fangs and dagger sharp talons. Giant hairy man-eating locusts with fangs, dagger sharp talons, and a really bad attitude. I made it a point not to look back.

Beside me, Bernie's breath was coming in gasping pants, but she didn't slow down. She seemed to have no trouble keeping up with me, which of course she shouldn't—I'm quick for my size, but longer legs are a significant advantage. She might be nuts, but she didn't panic, and she kept going. I approved of that. It showed good sense.

I wasted a moment trying to pull the strap the other way, then gave up and pulled the case all the way around, over my shoulder and down. I had just seized the case firmly in my hand and popped the snap open with my thumb when we took a corner a little too wide. Bernie caught her foot on one of the metal structures in the middle of the crossing and tripped. My hand tore out of hers as I stumbled along, wrenching my left arm and sending pains shooting up my neck from my shoulder blade, and I heard Bernie cry out as I went flying head first into the sand. Again.

The thrumming was closer, echoing crazily off of the stone walls and sounding like it was coming from all directions at once, but mostly from behind. My right arm and hand were buried beneath my torso, clutching the thingy with all my might, and I prepared to push the button even as my legs kept moving, driving my head into the sand, farther from whatever was making the noise, and farther from—

"Bernie," I yelled, trying to turn around, trying to get up, trying, in defiance of all good sense, to move *towards* the danger, while a little voice was screaming in my head, "You idiot! Plan A! Plan A! Push the button! Push it *now!*"

The noise grew louder. It sounded like giant steel locust wings vibrating ninety miles a minute. It sounded like enormous buzz saws cutting sheet steel. It sounded like death and destruction. And it sounded like it was on top of me.

I still don't know why I didn't just push the button and leave her there. I wanted to. She had shot at me, spied on me, hated me. I hadn't felt any qualms about leaving the other customers at Dino's to die under Viking axes. It just made sense. I would have died, too, if I'd tried to help them. I'd die now, if the thrumming caught me. I knew that. I should run away. Running away was what I did. That's what life had taught me.

I didn't want Bernie to die, mind you. But I didn't want to die either.

Behind me, Bernie was on her hands and knees, her face drawn in pain, the metal branch-work rising gracefully behind her. She was trying to get up, but it looked like she had sprained her ankle. The thrumming was louder still, almost deafening, and was now plainly echoing from the passage to the left. I was sure I was about to see whatever was making it, and I was almost rigid with fright. For a moment I looked Bernie in the eyes. I couldn't read what was in hers, except for pain...but I've no doubt that she could read what was in mine.

But even as I thought all this, even as my heart sunk and my bowels turned to water and my thumb quivered with the strain of *not* pushing the button, I got myself turned around; and feet skidding against the sand and the stone beneath, my right hand still clamped around the case, I scrambled along, nearly falling, only half-vertical, frantic in my haste. She stretched out her arm, still unable to rise, and I stretched my left arm, reaching, reaching, and the moment we locked hands my right hand clenched and I mashed my thumb onto the button.

There was a weird moment of exceeding timeliness and we came down with a thud on my mom's deep pile living room carpet.

There. All up to date, I thought with distant satisfaction. I was home, and Bernie was safe, and the giant steel demon locusts hadn't gotten us. There were voices in the kitchen and a growling in my stomach, but I couldn't attend to them. Sleep seemed like a much better idea. Sleep, yeah, that's the ticket...

"So, Michael, if you're done bleeding on my carpet I've got dinner ready."

Bleeding? I rolled over, ribs aching, and felt my right cheek carefully. It was abraded but not, I thought, gooey. "Yes," I said distantly, "I think I'm done. Thank you for asking." I climbed slowly to my feet, and felt the sand in my shoes. Nothing was chasing me; I could finally deal with it. Wiping at my eyes with one hand, I begin to sit down on the couch so that I could take my shoes off.

I heard Mom give me a look. "Not in here," she said.

I nodded. I'd made enough of a mess of Mom's living room already. I suppose I was rather a mess all by myself. I'm sure I brightened the tone of the room considerably when I got up and stumped out of it into the kitchen.

Bernie was sitting at the table with a mug of coffee. Her shoes were off, and her right ankle was wrapped in an Ace bandage. She smiled at me. Odd, that, since she seemed to be angry with me most of the time.

"Coffee, Michael?" asked Mom from behind me.

Coffee. Sure. I'd need a mug. I studied the table, blinking. There was another mug at the place next to Bernie. An empty mug. At my Mom's place. They'd been talking. For a while.

Oh, dear.

I kept my forebodings to myself.

"Yes, please," I said, and collapsed into the chair across from Bernie. Mom put a plate of home-made macaroni and cheese in front of me, and my hunger came back with a vengeance. I was halfway through the plate before she came back with the coffee. I expected her to tell me to slow down, and to remember that someone my size couldn't afford to eat like that, and that my youthful metabolism was going to fail me one of these days, but she didn't. Instead, when I'd cleaned the plate she took it and put another one just like it down in its place while I kept shoveling. I didn't even have to break my rhythm.

Meanwhile, Bernie kept smiling at me. It would have made me nervous if I'd had any attention to spare to it.

On the third plate I began to slow down, and alternated bites with sips of coffee. The coffee tasted good—a somewhat alarming fact, as coffee never tastes as good as it smells—and I could feel the caffeine beginning to take hold. As I ate, Mom and Bernie resumed their conversation.

"How many places did you go to?" Mom asked.

"Two, before we came back here. Neither of them were what you'd call vacation spots."

"And did Michael get anything to eat in between?"

"Well...sort of. I mean, it was *supposed* to be food. What it really was, I'm not quite sure. Have you ever heard of merchant oil?"

"Um. So, three transitions since last night?"

"I guess so, yes."

"I'd better get out the ice cream."

When I finished the third plate, Mom replaced it with an honest-to-goodness ice cream sundae, whipped cream and all. I stared at it for a moment, wondering how I'd ever get it down on top of three massive helpings of mac and cheese. And then my stomach rumbled so loudly that Bernie jumped, and seizing the spoon I buried my wonderment in vanilla ice cream and chocolate sauce. It was ever so much better than merchant oil—really, there's no comparison. Merchant oil is pretty much entirely unlike a chocolate sundae.

Bernie watched me eat in fascination.

"How can he do that? Does he have hollow legs?"

"It's the transitions," Mom said. "They take a lot of energy."

I didn't put down my spoon until the sundae was gone. There was a thin residue of ice cream and chocolate on the bottom of the bowl, and I considered trying to lick it up with my tongue. I also considered asking for seconds. There were no more untoward rumblings, though, and I thought better of it. Instead, I leaned back in my chair and took a deep breath.

Letting it out, I looked across at Bernie. "You OK?" I asked. She looked okay. Surprisingly okay, except for the Ace bandage.

"Yes, thank you. Your mom let me take a shower while you were sleeping. It helped a lot."

I nodded. "A shower. Yeah, I want me one of those." I shifted painfully in my seat. My arms and legs suddenly felt like they were made of lead. Lead wrapped in thick black velvet. "But maybe not just yet."

"And how are you?" Mom asked.

"Okay," I said with pointed untruth. "Mostly OK," I clarified. "Thanks for dinner. I needed that."

She nodded, but said nothing.

"So," I said, wondering how to put this. My mother clearly had hidden depths, and I wasn't sure how best to plumb them. She seemed to know a great number of things she had no business knowing. I mean, Moms do that, it's part of being a Mom, but this was beyond the usual. And then, she'd mentioned my father. She *never* talked about him, and had never been willing to answer any questions about him. I'd long since given up asking. I didn't remember him at all, and Mom had no pictures of him that I'd ever seen. I'd grown up with the feeling that fathers were something that happened to other people. Now Mom had raised the subject, and she certainly hadn't done so accidentally.

Finally, I said, "You, uh...you didn't seem particularly surprised to have us come tumbling into the living room like that."

"Oh, I was surprised," Mom said. "You made quite a thump.

But I wasn't perplexed. Joe McGillicuddy called from the Pancake Hut to tell me you and Bernie had disappeared during the fighting. It didn't seem likely that the Mongols had carried you off, so I figured you'd turn up here eventually." She pursed her lips, pondering. "So where did you get it? Was it from that fellow with the red mustache?"

I didn't bother asking what she meant by "it".

"That's right."

"Did he have anything to say about it?"

"Not much, being that he was already dead. We found it among his belongings."

"One of the Romans killed him," said Bernie. "We recognized him, and were trying to figure out how he did his disappearing act."

"Just as well that they did," said Mom, which shocked me. I mean, I knew Mom could be ruthless—the crossed arms, the tapping feet, the audible looks, you tell me. But she'd never struck me as bloodthirsty. "Can I see it?" she asked.

I pulled the case around in front of me, and took out the thingy. It was much easier to do, sitting at the table, than it was while running from giant hairy locust-winged man-eating Things That Cannot Be Named because I was fortunate enough not to have seen them. The thingy glowed a bit, then subsided when Mom took it. She turned it over in her hands, looking at it this way and that; then she shook her head. Whatever she was looking for, she hadn't found it. She handed it back to me and stood up, pushing her chair back. I slipped it back into its case.

"Wait a minute," she said. "I have something for you."

She hurried away; when she came back she was carrying a green metal box—the kind with a lock, that you keep cash in when you're selling candy bars and soda at high school football games. (When I went to the games, I was usually behind the counter, selling snacks—it was safer.) She put the box on the table, and sat down; then she put her hand inside the neck of her blouse, and brought out a small key on a chain. She pulled the chain over her head and handed it to me. "Your father wanted you to have this."

"Did he?" I said, leaving the question, "So why is this the first I've heard of it?" hanging in the air unsaid. Mom's tough, but she's always been good to me. Anyway, I was too tired to make a scene.

Mom heard it anyway, of course. She always did.

"I wasn't so sure it was a good idea," she said, looking straight at me. Not one to duck the issue, my Mom.

Bernie made as if to stand up. "I should be getting home," she said. "My parents must be horribly worried by now." So she still lived with her parents? I wondered why. But it sounded like an excuse. She looked a little embarrassed; I think she figured that if Mom and I were going to discuss family matters, she should make herself scarce.

"With the Mongols roaming the streets?" Mom said. "I don't think so. They haven't come up this street, but they've been going up and down the boulevard. I've seen them from my bedroom window."

"That close?" I exclaimed. "Should *we* be here, do you think?"

"I don't know where else we'd go," Mom said. "There was talk on the radio about a defensive perimeter and a shelter being set up at the high school, but I can't see that the high school is all that defensible. I thought I'd be just as safe here, as long as I kept the lights off after dark and didn't advertise my presence. There are a lot of Mongols, but not enough to do house-to-house searches of the whole town. And anyway, they seem to prefer the shopping districts." Her mouth quirked. "Besides, I was expecting you, and I didn't think you'd like to appear right in the middle of a crowd of people in the high school gym."

I shuddered. Perish the thought. I looked at Bernie.

"I think you'd better stay here," I said. Bernie frowned.

"But do call them," Mom said. "I should have suggested that before. I'm sorry. I sometimes get tunnel vision where Michael is concerned."

"So that's where he gets it," said Bernie.

"Half, anyway," said Mom. "The phone's over there, if you don't have your own."

I stared at the green metal box while Bernie made her call. I'd asked Mom why she wasn't surprised, and she'd responded with *this*. With something my father wanted me to have. What did that say about my father? I fingered the key impatiently. It was a perfectly ordinary little key, stamped out of sheet metal. I was eager to open the box, but to seemed rude to do it before Bernie came back, rather like beginning dinner before everyone was served. Had Bernie had anything to eat? I supposed she must have. I'd been too busy to notice.

"Hi, Mom, it's Bernie," Bernie said into the phone. "Yes, I'm OK. Yes, we got away from the Pancake Hut. It's a long story, but I'm fine. Where? Oh, I'm at Mrs. Henderson's. Michael's mother's house, yes. She says I'd best stay here. The Mongols, right. Uh-huh. What? Oh. Yes, I'll tell him. Bye, Mom. I love you." She put the phone down. She had an odd look on her face when she came back to the table.

"Mom says to tell you that Grandpa's going to rebuild his restaurant. Since you're one of his best customers, she thought you'd like to know."

I gulped. Fortunately, I was drinking coffee at the time, so it wasn't obvious. Did everyone in town know who I was? "That's nice," I said. "I'm looking forward to it."

Mom tapped on the box. "Open it," she said.

I unlocked the box with the little key, and then pushed at the little metal tab that unlatched it. It came open, revealing a tangled mess of black leather harness. It was finely tooled, and reminded me of the sturdy leather utility belts I'd seen policemen wear. I'd been unable to avoid studying them in my brushes with the law; when you're small for your age, a surprising number of things are near eye-level.

I pulled the harness out of the box, untangling it as I went. There were buckles and straps, and some kind of mass dangling in the middle of it. At last I had it all hanging in front of me.

What it was, I realized, was a shoulder holster. But it wasn't designed to hold a gun, oh no. The holster proper wasn't gun-shaped. It was disk-shaped, designed to lie flat against your side, and it closed with a snap.

The holster was heavy—there was something inside. It could have been anything, but under the circumstances, I knew what it had to be.

My father had left me a Thingy.

I laid the harness down on the table, unsnapped the holster, and pulled out what I found there. The Thingy was bigger and heavier than the one I'd gotten from Red Mustache, and disk-shaped rather than cylindrical. The metal body was a slightly different color than the other, but the markings were the same. Or, rather, they were entirely different, but they were clearly of the same kind. The button, which was located in the middle of one broad side, was black rather than silver.

As I took the Thingy in my hand its markings glowed blue, just like the ones on the other, but this time it was a blue so bright it filled the kitchen and left me with after-images hanging before my eyes. I'd rather been expecting some such response, but the extreme brightness caught me by surprise, and I nearly dropped it. I closed my eyes and put it down gently on the table. After a moment the glow faded so that it no longer lighted up the room.

"You'd best put it on," Mom said. "Your father hated to be without it."

It seems odd to me now, but it didn't even occur to me to ask why. It just seemed self-evident. Here was a Thingy, with a delightfully designed rig that would keep it always to hand. Of *course* I'd best put it on. It wouldn't do not to.

I wonder about that sometimes. But on the other hand, I still wear it.

I pulled the other Thingy's strap over my head, and laid in on the table. Then I reconsidered, and put the whole thing in my pocket. It didn't seem like something I should leave lying around.

Then I stood up and tried to make sense of my father's

shoulder holster. Of course the straps were absurdly long, but that's what buckles are for, right? I pulled at them, but couldn't seem to make my fingers do what I wanted them to do.

Mom started to rise, but Bernie beat her to it. "Oh, for goodness sake," she said. "Come over here." I walked around the table to where she was sitting, and handed her the harness.

As Bernie pulled on this strap and that and fitted the whole thing to my body I felt rather like a knight whose lady was buckling on his sword belt. It was an absurd thought, but it made me squirm. Knights went out looking for trouble. That's what knights were *for*.

Having a lady might be nice, though.

"Hold still," she said. "I can't do anything with you squirming like that."

Or, perhaps not.

"Your father had that specially made," Mom said. "He said he wanted to know where his finder was at all times, and that he didn't want to have to fumble for it if he needed it in a hurry."

"Amen to that," I said, thinking of the buzz-saw wielding locusts That Could Not Be Named. If they *were* locusts.

At last Bernie had the straps fitting snugly, with my father's Thingy in its holster conveniently placed just below my left arm pit. I must have looked a sight—she'd had to shorten the straps so much that the ends stuck out all over.

While Bernie was working, Mom had retrieved a pair of kitchen shears from the tool drawer. She handed them silently to Bernie, who grabbed them and made short work of the straps, leaving a modicum of excess length for future adjustments, if and when my youthful metabolism failed me. The rig felt odd, but solid. I thought I could get used to it. I reached for the holster without looking, to make sure I could get at it in a hurry, and felt something odd about it. I raised my arm and ducked my head to get a closer look. In addition to the holster's main opening, there was a small flap on one flat side, with its own snap. I unsnapped it and flipped it open, and there revealed was the button on the side of the Thingy, which remained firmly encased in leather. Cool! I could get at the button without risking the Thingy falling out, even if I was hanging upside down from a spray of purplish wrought metal.

"Did you say it was called a 'finder'?" I asked. "I've been calling it a 'Thingy'."

"'Finder' is what your father usually called it," Mom said. "Most of the time. When he wasn't being hifalutin'. When he was being hifalutin' he called it a MOAT."

"A moat?" said Bernie, "Like around a castle? Or like a mote in your eye."

"Neither," said Mom. "It's an acronym. He said it was a Meta-Ontological Acquisition and Transport device. MOAT."

"Meta-Onto-what did you say?" I said.

"Meta-Ontological Acquisition and Transport."

"That's hifalutin', all right." I thought about it. The "transport" part I'd seen for myself, and the "meta-ontological" part was Greek to me, or, I guess, Latin, so I passed over it to the "acquisition" part. "So in addition to taking me places, it can bring things to me?"

Mom shook her head. "Think 'target acquisition'. It finds things and takes you to them."

"Oh. So what about the 'meta-ontological' part?"

Mom paused before answering. "Michael, did I ever tell you how your father and I met?"

"Mom," I said with what I thought was commendable patience, "this is almost the first time you've even admitted that I had one." Bernie began to look uncomfortable again.

"I suppose that's true," Mom said. "I'm sorry. But I think about him daily." She looked down at the table, collecting herself. "Anyway," she said, a little too brightly, "We met in philosophy class. Did you know I was a philosophy major in college?"

"Now that," I said, "I knew. You've only mentioned it, oh, I dunno, two or three times a week for as long as I can remember. It was one of the high points of my life when you stopped pushing tomes at me."

Mom blushed. "I *like* philosophy. I wanted *you* to like philosophy."

"Yes," I said, "But that doesn't excuse giving the *Nichomachean Ethics* to a thirteen-year-old."

Mom gave me a Look, and turned to Bernie. "So there I was in class. Aristotelian Metaphysics. It was an upper-division class, so everyone in it wanted to be there, but most of them thought Aristotle was all washed up. That included the instructor."

"All washed up?" said Bernie.

"'Of historical interest only,'" Mom intoned in a stuffy, pompous voice. "But there was one fellow who disagreed. He thought Aristotle was the cat's pajamas. It made for a lively class. Sometimes I thought about bringing popcorn."

"And that was my father?" I asked.

"That was your father. It wasn't just that he liked Aristotle, it was more than that. He seemed to think it mattered. It wasn't just speculation to him. He took it as seriously as the mechanical engineer I was dating took structural dynamics."

My Mom had dated someone other than my father? Weird. It's weird to think about your mother dating to begin with. I didn't know where to look. But at that point the leaden, black velvet feeling began to creep from my shoulders up through my neck to my brain. I yawned extravagantly, and Mom checked herself.

"But we can talk about that tomorrow," she said. "Bernie, come with me; we'll make up the bed in the guest room. Michael, you're filthy. Take a shower before you go to bed."

When Bernie got up, she limped around to my side of the table, knelt down, and kissed me on my dirty abraded cheek.

"You could have left me there," she said softly. "You didn't." Then she followed Mom out of the room.

Chapter 10

The night passed quietly, with no Mongol incursions, Viking raids, galumphing beasts, or giant hairy nameless man-eating locusts. At least, none that disturbed my sleep.

Morning found us back in Mom's kitchen. My appetite, though within the bounds of normalcy, was still sizable, and I concentrated on the french toast and scrambled eggs before resuming the previous night's conversation. She'd said more about my father the previous night than I'd ever before heard, and taken things in stride that would have left most people speechless. I was beginning to wonder how well I really knew my Mom. I was also beginning to wonder what else she might have to tell me, and whether I'd like it.

Eventually I pushed my plate away. "So," I said, "You were telling us about meeting my father."

Mom got a faraway look. She rested her chin on her folded hands, elbows on the table, still holding her fork between two fingers.

"So I was," she said. "Give me a moment. There are things I want to tell you, and things I need to tell you, and things your father asked me to tell you when you were old enough, and things you need to know for your own safety. But there's no point in hitting you with it all at once."

She sat like that for several minutes, staring out the window into the early morning sunlight that dappled the back yard.

Bernie caught my eye and nodded at the plates. I must have looked blank, because she mouthed "The plates!" at me and pointed. Oh. So I stacked the plates and took them to the sink, and got us some more orange juice.

At last Mom spoke.

"Michael," she said, looking at me seriously, "your father was a Traveler. That's what he called himself, what he called people like him."

She saw my expression, and maybe Bernie's as well, because she grimaced. "Now you're getting the wrong idea," she said. "I don't mean that he was a rambler, a good-for-nothing who couldn't stay home for long. He was a Traveler."

This time I heard the capital "T". I sort of half-nodded, and she nodded back.

"That means, more or less, that he had a finder, and that he knew how to use it." Here she waved a hand at the finder in its holster under my left arm. "Or, I guess, it means that he *could* use it. Not everyone can. Very few people can. Did you let Bernie try to use that one?"

"He did," said Bernie. "He gave me the first push. But nothing happened." I nodded virtuously.

Mom's eyebrows rose. "Very good, Michael. I'm impressed. Anyway," she went on, "To be a Traveler you have to be the son of a Traveller. Or maybe the daughter, but your father said he'd never met a Traveller who was a woman." Bernie looked sour, but she held her peace.

"OK, so he was a Traveler," I said slowly, just to make sure I was getting it. "So he could travel in time and bring things back with him, like our late friend did with the Vikings."

To my surprise Mom laughed. "Actually, no. That's the last thing he could do, though I can see how you were misled. Our late friend couldn't do it either. Your father was a Traveler, Michael, not a Time Lord."

"Wait a minute," said Bernie. "What about the Romans? I talked to Gaius Valens for quite some time. He's from Julius Caesar's day, I know he is. I know my history."

"No," said Mom, "he's not. There might well have been a Roman centurion named Gaius Valens in Caesar's day, but your Gaius Valens isn't him. He's from some other world-line much like ours but where Caesar's day was delayed by about two-thousand years."

"World-line...you mean like some kind of parallel dimension?" I said.

Mom smiled ruefully. "I wish your father were here—that phrase drove him nuts. 'There's no such thing as a parallel dimension,' he'd say," she said, dropping her voice at least an octave. "'Can height be parallel to width? Of course not!' He'd get quite animated about it." Mom looked out the window, her smile still rueful. "I used to enjoy winding him up and watching him go."

After a moment she took a deep breath and turned back to me. "But in the sci-fi sense of the phrase, yes. 'World-line' was his term for it. Really, that's why he was here."

I looked at her, not understanding.

"Here in this world-line. In this world. In my philosophy class," Mom said. "He wanted to understand how it all worked. Most Travelers don't care, he told me. But he wanted to understand. He wasn't foolish enough to think that he could work it all out by himself. So he Traveled to a place where his questions would be answered, and that was here."

"To a class in Aristotelian Metaphysics? You must be joking!" I said. "Like that has anything to do with anything."

Mom shook her head. "Not a bit of it. Your father said that Aristotle gave him the best tools for understanding the things he was doing of anyone he'd ever heard of. Aristotle didn't have the whole story; he thought there was only one world-line. But he had the right foundation for your father to build on."

A penny dropped. I could almost hear it, *clink*, it dropped so hard. "So that's why you kept pushing me towards philosophy!"

"That's right," she said. "I pushed too hard, of course. That's the way it is with things you like. You push too hard, and your kids go do something else. At least I managed to steer you into software after that."

"Hey, I got interested in software all on my own. And anyway, what does software have to do with it?"

"You go on thinking that, dear," said Mom. Bernie stifled a giggle. Yes, they'd been talking. "But I knew you were going to need philosophy eventually, and computer programming is the next best thing."

I must have looked unconvinced.

"Oh, come now, Michael. What do you spend all day doing?" She cocked an eye at me.

"Well, I...."

"You spend all day designing intangible structures of thought, abstractions that you can't see, touch or taste, that are completely divorced from what most people would call reality, and that nevertheless have to be exactly right or they are worthless. It's like Applied Metaphysics."

"Humph," I said. "I give up. Okay, so what?"

"Last night, you asked what 'Meta-Ontological' meant. That's so what."

I made the "get on with it" motion with my hand. Turnabout, after all, is fair play.

"I told you last night that the finder helps you find what you're looking for, and takes you to it. That's why you ended up here, in my living room."

Bernie had been listening quietly, but now she looked side-long at me, an evil grin growing on her face. "You mean Michael wanted his mommy?" For a moment I was hurt—Bernie was just like all the girls I'd known in school. Then I remembered her kiss the night before, and felt better. So I crossed my arms and raised a sardonic eyebrow at her. Then I made a face and stuck out my tongue. Then I blushed, because in that moment in the Old City, stumbling towards her, reaching for her hand, deafened by that buzz saw wail, I really *had* wanted my mommy.

"I wouldn't have chosen to put it that way," Mom said, "but in fact yes, that's exactly what I mean. I'm one of Michael's anchors." We both looked at her in surprise.

"So you're saying," I said when my blush had gone away, "that I think about what I want, and push the button, and the finder takes me there?"

"Exactly. And that's the problem."

I frowned. Once again, Bernie was quicker on the uptake than I was.

"Oh," she exclaimed, eyes bright. "It's like those stories where the genie grants you three wishes. You get exactly what you asked for, but that may not be what you really wanted, and you might not like what comes with it. Oh, my."

Mom nodded. "Suppose you wanted a fortune in gold, and you asked the finder to take you to one. It can do it, no question. But it might still be in the form of ore, buried deep in a mountain in the middle of nowhere, with no one to help you dig it out. Or it might belong to a warlord who'd kill you as soon as look at you if he finds you nosing around his treasure room. Or it might be in a sunken ship at the bottom of an ocean somewhere."

All the hair stood up on my arms, and I shivered. "You're saying I need to be cautious."

Mom nodded again. "Your father used to say that there are old Travelers, and there are bold Travelers, but there are no old, bold Travelers."

"Seems to me I've heard something like that before."

"It's still true, though," she said.

"What happened to him, then?" I asked. "If he was so knowledgeable, and so cautious, what happened to him? Did he just disappear and not come back?" Did he run out on us, was what I wanted to ask, was what I had always wanted to ask, but I couldn't bring myself to say it out loud.

Mom sighed deeply. "He went to get you a finder," she said. "I don't know where or how. There aren't very many of them, he told me. No one knows how to make them, and the Travelers who have them don't generally want to give them up. Sometimes it's possible to find one without an owner if you know where to look, but otherwise you need to take one from someone else.

Anyway, he found one, and evidently someone objected."

"Its owner?"

"He didn't say."

I didn't like the sound of that. It was one thing to learn that I actually had a father; it was quite another to learn that he might have been a thief.

"Was it this one?" I asked, tapping my finder in its holster.

"No, that was his own." There was a ragged edge to Mom's voice that I'd never heard before.

"But then how..."

Mom buried her face in her hands.

Bernie and I looked at each other. She shifted uncomfortably, and jerked her head toward the door, looking me a question. I shook mine. She'd been with me in the Old City, and woke me up in the Red Desert before we were galumphed and then engulfed; she deserved to learn what it was all about. We waited.

"He came back one night," Mom said from behind her hands. "You were seven months old. He'd found a finder, he said, but some other Traveler was on the trail of it. He didn't dare lead him to you and me, but having found a finder he wasn't going to abandon it. So he left his finder with me, with instructions to give it to you when you were older, and vanished with the one he'd found. He said the other Traveler would follow that one, and that he'd be back when he could. If he could." Her voice was rough; I could tell she was only just keeping things together.

"The one I got from Red Mustache," I said, hesitantly, "is it the one he'd found?"

Mom shook her head, no.

"That was a long time ago," she said. "He might be dead. He might be stranded. I don't know. I'm still waiting." She clasped her hands on the table, and looked at me. "I'm still waiting, Michael."

I had to ask. I couldn't help myself.

"Do you think he...that he..."

"No. He didn't abandon us, Michael. He said he was coming

back, and your father never lied to me. He'd come back to me if he could. After all, I'm *his* anchor, too."

She stood up abruptly. "Excuse me, please." She went to the sink and busied herself with the dishes. Bernie touched my hand; her eyes were warm with concern.

When Mom had finished the washing up, she poured herself a mug of coffee and came back and sat down at the table with it. She seemed drawn into herself, but more in control.

"You've used that word twice now," I said after a while. "'Anchor', I mean."

Mom took a deep breath and closed her eyes. Apparently she wasn't as collected as I'd thought. She exhaled and looked at me.

"There are an infinite number of world-lines, Michael. There's anything you can imagine, and many things you can't. Lots of the world-lines are pretty much alike. Right now there are an infinite number of towns like ours in which Dino's place didn't burn down."

I nodded. It was a familiar enough idea in the kind of TV shows that used words like "parallel dimension."

"So suppose you traveled somewhere else, and you wanted to come home. How can you be sure you came back to right world-line? It would look just like the one you'd left. There are a million Dino Balduccis, a million-million Joe McGillicuddys."

I stared at her in shock. She was right. How *could* I know? How did I know that this was my home, that this was my mother? I looked at Bernie, and took her hand across the table. Bernie I could be sure of, because she'd been with me the whole time. She looked as horrified as I felt, and returned my grip with interest.

Mom smiled ruefully at us.

"I see you're getting the idea," she said. "But it's okay, Michael. It's true that there are an infinite number of Bonnie Tylers out there who never met your father, who never married a Traveler. But only one of them is your mother. I'm the only me."

"That's what you mean by an anchor," I said, recovering. I

loosened my grip on Bernie's hand.

She nodded. "Your father used to say that particulars are distinguished by their relationships."

We looked blank again.

She sighed. "I wish you'd taken to philosophy, Michael. It would make all of this so much easier." She drummed her fingers on the table, gathering her thoughts.

"OK," she said. "There are universals and particulars. 'Dog' is a universal. Our neighbor's dog is a particular. Got that?"

I nodded. "Dog is a class and Fido is an instance of that class. Got it."

"Sort of," she said. "In Aristotle's philosophy, that would mean that our neighbor's dog is unique. There's only one of him."

"But really," said Bernie, "There's only one of him in this world-line. But there are dogs just like him in many world-lines. Is that it?"

"Right. For Aristotle, particulars were singular things. In reality, though, any given particular is a dime-a-dozen.

"The thing is, the finder is good at finding universals, but it's lousy at finding particulars. Or, you might say, particular particulars. If you asked it to find Mr. McGillicuddy's Corvette, well, it would find you one. But there are lots to choose from. It might be in this world-line or it might not. But you've only got one mother."

"I think I get that," I said. "So my anchors are things that are important to me, important enough that I have a special relationship with them."

"People mostly," she said. "People have more being than most other things. Very few inanimate objects have enough being to make good anchors. And 'special' is the right word. Very special. According to your father, the relationship has to be 'ontologically significant'."

"Would you please stop that?"

"No," she said flatly.

"Humph. So what makes a relationship 'ontologically

significant'?"

"It has to be part of your very being."

"Like the parent/child relationship."

"The biological parent/child relationship.   That's the most common.   Or marriage."

I pondered that.   "Marriage is ontologically significant?"

"It is when you do it right," said Bernie.   I looked at her in surprise, while Mom nodded emphatically.   I wasn't sure what either of them meant, but I filed it away for later, because another horrifying idea had struck me.

"Wait a minute.   Are there millions of *me*, too?"   That was an appalling thought.   A million Michael Hendersons, all of them small for their age, all of them getting beaten up behind the gym.

"No, glory be," said Mom.   "You're what your father called a true singular.   There's only one of you in all of the world-lines. All Travelers are true singulars.   There are other true singulars, too, apparently, including some places.   Your father once mentioned a place he called the Old City."

I shared a look with Bernie.   Goose pimples raised up all over my arms.   Hers, too.

"What did he, uh, what did he say about it?" I said.

"He said every Traveler ended up there at least once."   She stopped, looking out into the back yard again.

"And?" I said, after a few moments.

"He said that sometimes they came back."

"Oh."   I cleared my throat.   "I don't think you need to worry about that any more.   I think we've been there.   And here we are!" I finished brightly.   It didn't seem to cheer her up much.

We sat for a while.   The dishwasher churned in the background, filling the silence.

"Before my father left that last time," I said, "Did he tell you anything else?"

"He said he wasn't sure when he'd be back.   He wasn't sure whether he'd be able to come back.   But he'd taken some steps to take care of us."

"What kind of steps?"

"Money, to begin with." She looked down, then looked at me. She looked nervous. "You have to understand, Michael, that there's no magic. Your father wasn't any kind of a wizard. But there are many worlds out there. Some of them have different rules than ours, and many have odd kinds of technology. Your father had an inquiring mind, and he'd picked up a few tricks here and there."

She looked down again, not meeting my eye.

"He said he wasn't sure he'd be here to give you the training you needed. He said he'd take steps to make sure you developed the right reflexes, the reflexes a Traveler needs to survive. Then he took you somewhere. A few hours later he came back."

I frowned, puzzled. I glanced at Bernie, whose eyes were suddenly wide as an owl's. She was looking at me...in fact, she was looking me up and down.

Another penny dropped—this one sounded more like a manhole cover—and I barely stifled a fair assortment of rude words. I stood up and waved at myself.

"This? He gave me this?"

"I'm not entirely sure," Mom said, still not quite meeting my eye. Which meant that she *was* entirely sure, she just couldn't prove it. I swallowed more rude words.

"Was he short? Did he look like this?" I asked with growing anger.

Mom looked even more nervous. "Well, he looked a lot like you, yes. But he was, um, taller."

"How much taller?" I demanded. In fact, I think I was shouting a bit.

"Over six feet, actually."

I spat out one of the rude words I'd been contemplating. Mom didn't flinch. That made me even angrier, and I spat out another one. It was incredible, but I found I had no problem believing it. My own father had done this to me. I got up and paced around the kitchen. My father had bloody well cursed me! The swine! I'd never heard of such a thing. How could he have done that? I'd never heard of such a thing, I'd...

I stopped, and said the word again. I *had* heard of such a thing. I rounded on my mother.

"How nice," I said with bitter sarcasm. "He took 'steps'. Damn it, Mom, why didn't he just go the whole hog, and name me Sue along with it?"

At last Mom met my eyes. Her eyes were filled with apology and sympathy and unhappiness. I almost didn't recognize her.

Bloody hell. Well, know I knew why Mom hadn't wanted to give me my father's finder. It would only have led to questions, and questions would have led to explanations, and explanations would have led to—

"I think the whole idea was to teach you how to get *out* of trouble, not to get you into it," she said weakly.

"Great," I said, "Just great." Bernie's eyes followed me as I stomped out of the room.

Chapter 11

They let me brood until after lunch. I had dry Cheerios for lunch, and then I brooded some more. A few years ago after an exceptionally well-paying job I bought a really big chair for my desk, with all kinds of knobs and levers and things. It's a great chair for working in. If you pull the lower-right lever, the one that you can not only pull up and down but also slide in and out, it tilts backward quite a ways, and then it becomes a great chair for brooding in. In fact, it becomes not much good for anything else, since I can't reach anything on the desk from that position. So I held the box of Cheerios in my lap, and got crumbs all down my front. When I was done, my t-shirt was fortified with eight vitamins and minerals.

Some people brood over alcohol; I brood over Cheerios. It's cheaper, and has fewer after-effects, and the sales clerks don't look at me funny when I buy Cheerios. Also, after the events of the past week there was nothing else in the cupboard. I brooded over that for a while, too. I spent about half-an-hour brooding over whether I could use my finder to hop to some other world-line where there were groceries, and if I could, whether I could bring back enough food to have any left over after having eaten enough to make up for having jumped there and back, and whether I'd be attacked by Zulu warriors while I was shopping.

I concluded that (1), I could certainly do it, and that (2), if Red Mustache could manage a longship then I could manage a cart of groceries, and that (3), Red Mustache was dead and so Zulu warriors were unlikely. I was on the verge of beginning to think about getting up and maybe trying it when I started thinking about merchant oil and the whole plan came crashing to the ground. It simply wasn't worth it if I ended up at a grocery store full of things like merchant oil. Besides, there'd probably be Red Indians, and when I got back, scalped, nibbled on by the Nameless Locusts, lacerated by flying buzz-saws and half-drowned because the grocery store the finder took me to was in a shipwreck at the bottom of an ocean somewhere, there would be Mom, and Bernie, and they'd kill me.

Worse. They'd probably both cross their arms at me at once.

I almost started thinking about why Red Mustache had gone to so much effort to import "ancient" warriors into our town, but that would have been constructive.

Then I began to wonder what day it was, because I'd lost track. That took me another fifteen minutes or so. It was Wednesday evening when I went to the Pancake Hut for dinner, and I'd slept twice since then, so it had to be Friday. I could have found out in a couple of seconds by clicking on the mouse and waking up my computer, but then I'd have had to tilt the chair forward, and that would have interfered with my brooding.

You might be surprised to find out that I wasn't brooding over my father and what he'd done to me. In fact, I was. But I was an old hand at brooding over my height, and his betrayal just added a painful garnish to the basic dish. I found I could brood about *that* at a deep level, while my conscious mind was brooding about less important things...or, for a good bit of the morning, about nothing at all. I'm a skilled brooder, I am. I have practice.

Besides, it hurt too much to think about.

Anyway, I guess it was a little after one o'clock when I heard footsteps coming up my stairs, followed by a knock. Not a quiet little knock, but a good, solid, nothing to hide, please-come-to-the-door-I-know-you're-in-there kind of knock.

I stayed in my chair. That was the only door, and the windows either didn't open or there was no easy way to the ground, so

Plan A was out. I'd have to do something about that. Later.

The knock was followed by a louder knock. That meant it was Bernie. Mom would have just crossed her arms and waited, and then I'd have had to go open the door. Mom can cross her arms more expressively than anyone I know.

"Michael?"

Yup. Bernie. I wished she'd go away; she was interrupting my brooding. Interrupted brooding turns into sulking, and sulking is an ugly thing. No one wants to be around a sulker. Better just to stay away.

I ate another handful of Cheerios.

"Michael! Let me in."

Nope, I thought. Not gonna do it. Anyway, the door was unlocked. With luck she wouldn't notice.

No such luck. I heard the latch turning and the door creaking open, and I imagine she stuck her head in. She couldn't see me of course. My chair is not only good for brooding in, it also has a high back, making it good for hiding in.

"Michael Henderson!" she said. I was lucky she didn't know my middle name. "There's only one door, so you can't run. I know you're in here, so you can't hide for long. If you don't want to hurt my feelings and prove your mom right at the same time, you'd better move on to Plan C pretty darn quick."

Humph. This is what comes of telling girls about your plans. They use them against you. Bernie reminded me of one cute little girl I'd known in second grade, before I was small for my age. She—but the less said about that, the better. I sighed, and turned the chair around with a languid kick to the lower-right desk drawer.

"Yeah?" I asked as ungraciously as I could manage, which was considerable. Brooding isn't conducive to good manners. Then I sulked at her.

"Hah!" she said, smirking in triumph as she closed the door behind her. "Your mom said you wouldn't talk to me."

Plan C, huh? Direct action against the enemy. I thought about that. Knocking her to the floor seemed uncalled for, given that she wasn't pointing a gun at me. Besides, it was trite. It had been overdone. It was becoming a habit.

Driving right through her to the door would mean either going into the house with my Mom, or out into the street with the Mongols. And anyway, it would mean getting out of my chair.

"Have you eaten anything?" she asked.

So physical action was out. That meant something in the verbal line, and I sighed again. That's another problem with girls: they're verbal. That left me doubly handicapped. Still, I gave it my best shot.

"You're wrong, you know," I said.

She looked quizzically at me.

"I could have run. I could have pushed the button, and poof!"—I made poofing motions with my fingers—"I'd have been gone. Maybe you'd never see me again."

She took this sally in stride. "On the other hand, your mom also said that even if I could get you to talk, you probably wouldn't say anything to the point. Now, have you eaten?"

Darn. Well, her stride was much longer than mine. I tried again.

"Yes," I said.

She looked me over, taking in the box of Cheerios, and I imagine, the crumbs.

"Yes, I see that you have," she said. "In that case, may I sit down?"

There seemed to be nothing to say to this. She clearly wasn't going to leave until she'd had her say, and if I was nasty about it she'd just invoke her feelings and my Mom's expectations again. So I grunted, and she sat down comfortably in my one overstuffed chair as though I'd invited her to make herself at home. She didn't settle into it for a social chat; she was leaning forward, poised, ready for action. She was a Woman with a Mission.

"First of all," she said, "I'd like to tell you what I think of your father. He's a Grade A, Number One—", she began, and her discursions thereafter took on his parentage, his parenting skills, his and morals, with digressions on his likely interests and vices, his personal habits, his faults, both venial and mortal, his virtues, notable mostly by their absence, and her wishes for his prolonged stay in purgatory. I have to say, she had a good grasp of invective. She went on for a good twenty minutes without repeating herself once, and without using any words she'd have to apologize for afterwards. She got quite heated about it. Apparently her ankle felt better; even before she was up to full steam she was back out of her chair, striding back and forth, waving her hands and shooting me angry looks.

No; I'm being unfair. She looked at me, and she had an angry look on her face. She wasn't shooting the angry looks at *me*. I was grateful.

It made me tired, watching her stride about like that. And I found it irritating, in an equivocal sort of way. On the one hand, I'd been thinking most of the same things for most of the morning. On the other hand, it's never pleasant to hear someone else abusing the father you've only just learned you had, especially when they do it so emphatically. And on the third hand, it was mildly entertaining, and I was in no mood to be lifted out of my brooding.

By the time she ground to a halt, I was thoroughly irritated. "Where do you get off, coming up here and bothering me and saying nasty things about my father?"

She loomed down at me with angry eyes. "Damn it, Michael, he was a skunk, and you know it!"

That was too much. I jumped out of my chair and did my best to loom back up at her. "Will you sit down!" I shouted. She sat down demurely, and if there was a note of triumph in her eyes I quite failed to detect it.

When she had sat down, and I could look daggers straight across at her without craning my neck, I went on.

"So he was a skunk," I shouted, "but you're not being remotely fair."

"Not fair?" she shouted back. She looked to be winding herself up for another tirade, but I cut her off.

"Not fair! You have him taking candy from babies and depriving widows and orphans of their livelihood. Whatever he did," I trailed off weakly, "he didn't do that." And then I sat back down in my chair, and curled up, and didn't look at her.

After a strained silence Bernie got up and knelt down by my chair.

"I'm sorry, Michael," she said, softly. "I get carried away. But he makes me so mad, your father. He took care of you, all right. Those plans of yours, A, B, and C? Those are the reflexes he wanted you to develop, aren't they?"

"Yeah, I think they must be." I tried not to sniffle. "You have to admit," I said, "it worked."

"Those are great reflexes. Absolutely perfect—when you're caught behind enemy lines." She sighed. "But it's no way to live when you're at home, Michael. It's pathological."

I turned my head to look at her, where she knelt on the carpet. For once I had to look down at her. She looked back up at me, her face earnest and full of concern. I didn't know what to say. I wasn't used to solicitude from pretty girls my own age—at least, not once they realized that I was their own age—and it flustered me. And anyway, prolonged brooding makes it hard to think clearly.

"And it's no way to take care of your family, either. Your father was a damned coward, Michael." She stopped, and looked embarrassed. "I'm sorry," she said. "I hope he isn't that. But he threw away his whole life with you. If he had stayed, if he had fought for you, he'd have seen you grow up, and you'd have had a father, and you wouldn't have been like this."

I found myself getting angry again.

"Like this. Stunted." I said bitterly, waving at my little body. "Is that what you're saying?"

Then she did say a rude word. And then, while I was still reacting to it, she went on. "Sure, call yourself stunted, if you like. As if your size matters," she said. "You had to be some size, after all."

Stunted, I thought. It wasn't my size she was concerned about. It was me. The rest of me. Swell.

My anger ebbed. My throat was sore from the yelling, and I found myself remembering my manners.

"Can I get you something to drink," I asked, only half-grudgingly.

She took that in her stride, too. "Yes, please," she said. I couldn't get up with her kneeling there, so she sat back cross-legged. "What do you have?" She flipped her hair back over her shoulders.

"Water, diet soda, and milk." I considered, remembering the state of my larder. "*Chunky* milk. I don't recommend it."

"Water," she said.

I got a bottle of water for her, and a soda for me, and sat back down in my chair. It was nice to look down at someone. I tilted it forward, though.

"OK, we've established that my father was a skunk. Did you have anything else on your mind?"

"The Mongols, Michael." She was looking earnest again, and worried. "What are we going to do about the Mongols?"

I stared at her in dismay. "We? What do you mean, we? Can't they call in the National Guard, or something?"

She shook her head. "Budget cuts, they say. Your mom and I have been listening to the radio. And I don't think anyone outside of town believes it, anyway. I mean, Mongol hordes? Here? So we're on our own. But anyway, you're missing the point."

I was still rattled. "So what's the point?" I had a big gulp of the diet soda. Caffeine and diet sweetener. The staff of life.

"How many Mongol riders did you see at Foodland?"

"I dunno...maybe ten or twelve. I wasn't in a counting mood."

"And how many at the #1 Market?"

"About the same; maybe fewer."

"And how many riders attacked the Pancake Hut?"

"It was dark," I said. "How should I know?"

"More than a dozen?"

I thought about it. "Yeah, probably."

"A lot more?"

"Could be," I said, still puzzled.

"Where did they come from?"

I continued to stare at her. "Red Mustache brought them, of course."

"Before or after the Romans killed him?"

"Well, before, of course—wait a minute. What are you saying?"

"The police have counted over two hundred of them, and more are showing up all the time. They've pretty much taken over the business district. And they've set up an encampment in Corey Park, and the police can't get near it." She shrugged.

"So," she said, "Where are they coming from?"

The Mongols...or were they Mongols? According to Mom, they weren't real Mongols any more than Gaius Valens was a real Roman. Pseudo-Mongols? Or maybe Valens *was* a real Roman. If he wasn't a real Roman, then what was he?

I decided to continue calling them Mongols.

What I wanted to say to Bernie's question was, "Why ask me? How should I know?" But I didn't. I mean, it was obvious why me. If the Mongols were still arriving, then Red Mustache must have a partner, or a rival, or an enemy. There was some other Traveler involved. If you have to fight fire with fire, then I was the only guy in town with a match. But I didn't like it.

"Bernie, do I look like a knight in shining armor?" I heard a bit of a whine in my voice, and I winced. She opened her mouth to speak, and I raised my hand. "And can we cut the yelling? I've had a bad morning, and my head aches."

She stopped, took a deep breath, and said, "Michael, people are dying. The riders are starting to move out into the residential neighborhoods. This town wasn't built for defense; there's nowhere to hold the line against them. We need to cut them off at the source."

"So you *do* want me to be a knight in shining armor. I suppose you want me to hop right on down to Corey Park and see what's going on."

"Michael, you are so dense sometimes. It's only in the movies that the intrepid kid saves the world all by himself. And anyway, you're not a kid, even if you do dress like one."

"These are the clothes that fit," I said hotly. "Intrepid kid. I suppose you're trying out for the role of plucky girl sidekick?"

Bernie tensed, and just as it was beginning to look like there'd be more yelling, despite my aching head, the phone on my desk rang. I took a deep breath, and took the call; it was probably one of my clients, wondering when the current project would be done. I used the speaker phone; maybe Bernie would take the hint and go away. I was wrong on both counts.

"Hello?"

"Michael?" came a voice. It sounded familiar, but I couldn't quite place it.

"Yes? Can I help you?"

"On the contrary! This is Joe McGillicuddy. I called your mother to see if you'd gotten home safely, and she suggested I call you; she said you could maybe use some help." I glanced at Bernie; she was smirking again. I gave her a look that should have melted steel, but it bounced off of her dark brows and blue eyes. The ricochet nearly killed me.

Somehow I managed to keep all of this out of my voice. I *am* a professional, and I have the telephone manner to prove it.

"Thank you, Mr. McGillicuddy. How did your Corvette come through the battle?"

"Call me Joe, please, Michael, you're not in my class anymore." He paused, then, "Well, between the Romans and the Mongol hordes, that 'vette's pretty much a goner," he said. "Hoof prints, and broken windows, and arrows in the upholstery, not to mention the dents when they moved it into the barricade." There was a pause, during which I maintained a respectful silence. "We fought them off, though," he went on more cheerfully. "I think I might get one of those Hummers. An H1, not one of those hifalutin' H2's. Now there's a vehicle with *authority*."

My brain was starting to come on-line again.

"Interesting you should mention Hummers, Joe," I said. "I guess I need something looked into. These Mongols—apparently there are more of them all the time."

"That there are, Michael."

"I need to know where they are coming from."

"Mongolia, maybe?"

"No, no. I mean, they must be appearing somewhere, like the Romans did outside the Pancake Hut. It's like, here today, gone tomorrow, only backwards. I need to know whether they are just appearing in dribs and drabs, here and there, or whether there's one particular place they are showing up. Do you suppose you and Brother Bear could go looking around and maybe find out?"

"Brother who?"

"Brother Bear—you know, the guy with the Hummer."

"Oh, you mean Alex Schafer. 'Brother Bear'—I like that. He will, too. It suits him." There was a pause, as he considered. "Might be a bit dangerous for Alex and I just to go riding around in the Hummer, but maybe I can work something out with Guy." I could almost hear him nod decisively. "Sure, we'll find out for you."

"Who is Guy?" I asked.

"Guy Valens. You know, the centurion. I tell you, once those Romans form a shield wall, the Mongols just bounce off."

"You can talk to him?"

Joe chuckled. "Before I retired here and started rebuilding my 'vette, I was a classics professor at the university. Before that I was a Marine. I guess my accent's atrocious, but yeah, Guy and me, we understand each other."

A Marine who spoke Latin. My universe was expanding every day. "Thank you," I said.

We exchanged cellphone numbers, and then he said, "How did you get free of the Pancake Hut, anyway?"

"It's a kind of knack I've got, Joe. I'm sorry to have abandoned you."

"Not to worry. The same sort of knack the fellow that brought in those Vikings had, maybe?"

"Something like that."

"Thought so. Did you get that pretty blonde away safely, too?"

I looked at Bernie, who blushed. So did I. Humph, I thought. He'd been talking to Mom; I'm sure he knew perfectly well that I had, and who Bernie was, and probably had a shrewd idea that she was in the room listening to our conversation.

"Yes, Joe, I did."

"Good. She's a keeper, and don't you forget it. I'll be in touch."

He hung up, and I pushed the button to terminate the call on my end.

"There," said Bernie, who was still blushing. "Was that so hard?"

Chapter 12

"There's always treasure hunting," I said.

"Sure," said Bernie. "Now tell me how that's different than stealing, hmmm?"

"Oh, come on. I don't want to steal from anyone. An infinite number of worlds, there must be lots of treasure lying around that doesn't belong to anyone."

With nothing to do until we heard from Joe and Brother Bear, Bernie and I had settled down to wait. First, I had repositioned my chair so that I could see out the window and down the driveway. If any Mongols came to pay a visit, I wanted to see them coming. Second, I had retrieved Bernie's grandfather's pistol from under the couch. I didn't know anything about how to use it, beyond what everybody thinks they know, but I felt better for having it handy. After that, we had fallen into an extended conversation over microwave popcorn and soda. (I'd had to go downstairs to Mom's to get the popcorn.) We'd talked about growing up small, if "up" is the right word, about growing up Catholic, about living in a small town, about each other. Most of that is none of your business. Eventually, we'd worked our way around to what might be called the commercial possibilities of being a Traveler.

"And why doesn't it belong to anyone?" said Bernie. "Because it's at the bottom of the sea, or in the middle of a nuclear wasteland, or buried in a hole in land that belongs to somebody who doesn't know it's there, which makes it stealing again."

"So it has to be inaccessible. Maybe it's in a remote geographic location. Or maybe it's in a world where nothing lives, like the Old City."

Bernie shivered.

"Well, OK," I said, "Maybe the Old City isn't a good example."

"I think it's a great example," said Bernie. "If there's nothing living there anymore, maybe there's a good reason."

I grimaced. I could still hear that buzz-saw thrumming in my ears, any time I cared to think about it. "Yeah, could be," I said. "So what about diamonds? I understand that at some of the diamond mines in South Africa, the rough diamonds were originally found just lying about."

Bernie nodded thoughtfully. "That could work. You take a pail and a shovel and a backpack, and bring back a fortune in uncut diamonds. And then you try to sell them, and you've got De Beers and everyone else in the industry hiring private detectives to follow you about and discover how you stole them from their mines, or where your new mines are. If you're looking for a quiet life, you might want to think again."

I smirked. It felt good; I'd been the recipient of too many smirks, recently, and it was time to even the score.

"You're thinking too small again. If there are an infinite number of worlds, there are infinite worlds in which the Kimberly diamond mines are still unknown, and there are also infinite worlds in which to sell the diamonds. I don't need to sell them here."

She smirked back. "And you're not thinking at all. So you take your diamonds somewhere else and sell them. And you get paid in the local currency: Carthusican zlotnicks, or something like that. Where are you going to spend them?"

"Nope," I said, seeing her smirk and raising her one. "Dollars. Good old American dollars. There must be tons of world-lines just next door."

"Uh-huh. Where you've got all the same problems selling

them as you would here. And then the money isn't *quite* identical and you get arrested for counterfeiting. No thank you."

At that point my cell phone rang, which was just as well. It was Joe McGillicuddy. I put him on speaker, and Bernie and I huddled around it.

"Joe! Where are you?"

He laughed. "You'll never believe it. We're at Brother Bear's girl-friend's apartment."

"Uh, OK. How come?"

"She lives about a block away from Corey Park, and was getting really nervous about all of the little guys on horses racing around in the streets. It's the kind of building with electronic security gates all over, so she hasn't had any trouble so far, but Brother Bear kind of wanted to keep an eye on things."

Brother Bear certainly had the right, and maybe even the duty, to take care of his girl friend, but I needed information. I was trying to find a polite way to express my frustration without offending Joe, when he laughed again.

"Now, I know what you're thinking," he said. "Don't worry, we haven't forgotten what you asked us to do. We've got a couple of pairs of high-powered binoculars, and did I forget to mention? Brother Bear's girlfriend has a really nice view of the park. The Romans are down in the garage, Brother Bear and Guy are up here with me, we can see what the little buggers are doing, and Mary Claire's feeling ever so much more relaxed. It's all good."

"So what can you see?" asked Bernie.

"That you, Miss Balducci?"

"Yes, it is, Mr. McGillicuddy."

"Oh, call me Joe, please. Good for you, Michael." I blushed. As if he hadn't known. "Anyway, what we can mostly see is a whole lot of mud and a whole lot of Mongols. Those horses of theirs have trampled the grass into mush all over the park. There are campfires, and riders patrolling the outskirts. There are patrols coming and going all the time."

"How many Mongols can you see?" I asked.

"I count four or five hundred, and you're right—there are more all the time."

"Can you tell what direction the newcomers are coming from?"

There was a pause. "That's the crazy thing, Michael. We've got spotters all around the park now, and we've been keeping watch for several hours. That whole time, the number of riders leaving the park and the number coming back has been fairly constant. But there are more Mongols in the park now than there were when we started."

"So they are appearing inside the park itself."

"That's what it looks like."

OK, I thought, so our rogue Traveler was in the park somewhere, protected by half-a-thousand vicious killers. Happy happy, joy joy. I sighed.

"Can you tell me more than that?" I asked.

"I can, but I'll tell you, Michael, it's hard to believe. If I didn't have an honest-to-gosh Roman standing here beside me, I wouldn't believe it myself, and it's happening right here in front of me."

"Joe?" said Bernie.

"Yes, Miss Balducci?"

"It's Bernie. Joe, Michael and I experienced six impossible things before breakfast yesterday. Can you get on with it, please?"

"Yes, Ma'am! Well, what it is, is they are appearing out of nowhere right in the middle of the park. You know that open space in front of the bandshell?"

"Yes, we know," I said. I wanted to make the "get on with it motion" with my hand, but Joe wouldn't have been able to see it. Bernie crossed her arms. He didn't notice that, either.

"Well, there's something there that didn't used to be there. It's a square platform a few inches high and maybe eight feet square. It's kind of a mottled purple color. The Mongols are appearing on it, with their horses. Each time one appears, the whole thing glows blue."

"Purple and blue!" said Bernie.

"Joe," I said, "Let me guess. Does it look like old corroded brass, only purple instead of green?"

"Now that you mention it, yes. That's exactly what it looks like. It looks broken, too."

Bernie and I looked at each other. "Broken how?" I asked.

"Well, the platform is mostly flat, but not quite. It looks like something really big stepped on it, maybe. And there are two posts rising from the corners on one side, but they look broken off. They have different heights, and the tops look jagged. They look kind of like fancy wrought iron, with all different kinds of branches twining and twirling about. Except that they are purple, of course."

"Do you see anybody leaving? Anybody stepping onto the platform and disappearing?"

"No, not so far."

"How fast are they coming through?" asked Bernie.

"A new one shows up every few minutes. They must have a regular line up at the other end."

The other end—that was the rub. I frowned.

"Joe, we're going to need to think about this for a bit. Can you stay there and keep an eye on things?"

"Absolutely, Michael. Mary Claire has a pizza in the oven, and there's cold beer in the fridge. We're all set."

"Good for you. I'll be in touch."

"No worries. I'll call you if anything new happens."

I terminated the call, and Bernie and I looked at each other.

"That's not a rogue Traveler," she said. "That's a gate."

There's a software development maxim that usually comes in handy at times like this: if all else fails, Read The Fine Manual. Unfortunately, the gate's manual, assuming there was one, was in the hands of the Mongols. I thought it likely that the gate was akin to a finder; but I didn't have a manual for one of those, either. My next stop when faced with something outside my experience would usually be Wikipedia, but I was confident that

I'd find nothing there that was either helpful or to the point. That left searching out a relevant authority—so we went downstairs and talked to Mom. Bernie and I quickly filled her in.

Mom listened carefully, and then shook her head.

"No," she said. "Your father never mentioned any such thing as a gate. In fact, I think he'd have said it was impossible. Are you sure no other Traveler is involved?"

"Of course not," I said. "But we know Red Mustache is dead, and anyway I have his finder." I did, too. My father's was in its holster under my arm, and RM's was in my pocket. Somehow, I didn't want to leave it lying around somewhere. "He might have a partner, but if so we've not seen any sign of him." Well, we'd seen the Explorer in the Old City, but there was no reason to think that he was mixed up in all this.

"But we *have* seen something like the platform that Joe described to us," said Bernie. "It sounds like it's made of the same kind of metal as the things we saw in the Old City."

"More than that," I said. "It glows blue, just like a finder. And there's another connection to the Old City." I told them about the carved panel and the blue flash I thought I'd seen just before I'd fallen on Bernie.

"You didn't mention that before," said Bernie.

"I wasn't sure I'd seen it before," I said. "And anyway, I was a bit distracted."

"Maybe this 'gate' is a device that lets a Traveler send people to another world-line without going himself," Mom suggested.

I considered that.

"Could be," I said. "There almost has to be something at the other end that's sending the riders across. It could be a Traveler, or it could be another gate, maybe another platform like the one in the park. That would make it more like a bridge." Mom and Bernie both nodded. "But that still leaves the question of where the other end is."

"Not here, at any rate." Mom said. "Not in this world-line, I mean. When you Travel, you Travel between world-lines. That's just how it is."

"So I can't use my finder to bop down to the store, then?"

"Not any store where they already know you, at any rate," said Mom.

"Pity. It would have saved wear and tear on my bike."

Mom didn't even dignify that with a look.

"So how do we find the other end?" asked Bernie. "We can't just use the finder to find us some Mongols—they probably wouldn't be the right ones. And wherever the right Mongols are, Michael doesn't have any anchors there."

"If you knew what the thing at the other end was," Mom said, "you could have your finder take you to something of that kind. But you don't know what it is, and even if you did it wouldn't necessarily be the right one." She pondered. "Maybe you could use the platform in the park as a kind of reverse anchor? There's got to be a relationship between it and whatever is at the other hand, and if the platform is like a finder, it's probably a true singular. You could try to find the particular thing that's connected to it. But again, you'd have to know what you were trying to find."

"If it's a bridge," said Bernie, "the other end is probably a lot like this end. It would be worth a try, anyway."

"But I'd have to get near the one in the park. No, thank you," I said.

Mom nodded. "Smart boy. I don't see how you can do it without getting killed."

Bernie slammed her chair back, unable to contain her frustration. "But if we can't figure out where they're coming from, how are we going to find out what they're up to? And how are we going to stop them?"

"You might try asking one of them," said Mom, mildly.

"But..." I began, and then felt like hitting myself on the head. The finder had let me understand Gaius Valens and the Explorer; it ought to let me understand the Mongols as well.

"That almost seems like cheating," said Bernie.

"Hey, any port in a storm," said Mom.

* * *

That left us with just two problems: acquiring a Mongol to talk to, and persuading him to cooperate with us. About the second, I found I had some ideas. About the first, well, I just called Joe on my cell phone.

"Michael! What can I do for you?"

"Anything new going on in the park?"

"There's more of 'em, but other than that, no. I said I'd call you if anything changed."

"Yeah, I know. Look, I need another favor. I need to talk to one of the Mongols."

"Talk to one? How are you going to do that? They don't speak English." He paused. "At least, I don't think they do."

"That's my problem. I talk to computers for a living; I ought to be able to manage a Mongol. But anyway, can you get one for me?"

"You mean capture one?"

"Yeah."

"Probably, but it might not be necessary. Let me make some phone calls."

He rang back about ten minutes later. I turned on my phone's speaker and put it in the middle of the table.

"I've got a live one for you," he said. "The cops arrested one of the Mongols Wednesday evening, before there were so many of them running around. He's still in a cell down at the Wilson Street station."

Oh, joy, I thought. A police station. Not only was I going to have to confront a smelly, murderous, pony-riding psychopath, I was going to have to do it in Bully Central. I knew Bernie was watching, though, so I braced myself.

"Any chance you and your guys could get me down there safely?" I asked.

"No need. Chief Roderick's sending a squad car to pick you up." I could hear Joe grinning. "The chief's a buddy of mine. You'll get there in one piece."

"Thanks, Joe, I'll let you know how it comes out," I said, and ended the call.

Double joy, I thought, putting the phone in my pocket. I was going to get to ride in a police car. What fun.

In the end it wasn't one police car; it was four. Safety in numbers, I guess: my own private motorcade. The officer who came to the door was a young guy, probably no older than I was, with a buzz cut and abnormally large pecs. He looked like a recruiting poster. I didn't like him.

I also didn't like the way he looked at Bernie as he helped her into the back of his squad car. He didn't offer to help *me*, I noticed, although I was the one who was burdened—I'd run upstairs and packed my laptop into its case while we were waiting. I had a cunning plan, and the laptop was part of it.

Officer Recruiting Poster's partner was behind the wheel.

"We won't cuff you this time," he said as I climbed in. He smiled at me through the metal screen, an expansive kind of smile in a face that looked like it spent lots of time in donut shops. Have I mentioned that I don't spend any time in donut shops?

"Nice of you," I said. "By the way, we need to stop at the library."

"The library," said Officer Doughboy. "Have you got any idea what the streets are like? We didn't bring four cars for the fun of it."

"The library," I said. "I'm sure you can manage, and there's something I need to get."

Officer Recruiting Poster shrugged. "If you say so. The chief said to do whatever you needed. Any library in particular?"

"One that's not overrun by Mongols would be my preference," said Bernie. "Why the library, Michael?"

"I need to pick up some DVDs," I said. "Previews of coming attractions."

"I'll see what I can do," said Officer Doughboy. He got on the radio and explained the situation to the officers in the other cars, and our motorcade got under way.

Chapter 13

The streets were empty of cars and pedestrians, and most of the businesses were closed and dark. That included both of the public libraries we drove by, and so we were on our way to a little video rental place Doughboy knew where the owner lived in an apartment over the shop, when we had our only brush with the Mongols. We were heading east on Nova Scotia approaching the intersection of Abrams when a small troop of Mongols rode into the intersection from the north and spread out, blocking our way. I expected Doughboy to turn the car around; instead he accelerated. The cars behind us did the same.

"What are you doing?" I said, with some asperity; I didn't shriek, no matter what Bernie says.

"Not to worry," said Recruiting Poster. "We've done this before." His words were breezy, but his tone was grim.

The riders watched us coming, faces stony, sitting their ponies; their ponies did much the same. I'd have thought that the ponies would have had more sense, but perhaps they were more afraid of their riders than they were of us. The riders had their bows out, but they didn't fire.

"Arrows just glance off." said Doughboy. "They've learned not to waste them."

Then, when we were about fifteen feet from the line of ponies, just as Bernie and I was bracing myself for the inevitable collision, the Poster turned on the siren while Doughboy sounded the horn. The ponies shied and danced out of the way, their riders struggling to control them. I think we winged one—at least, there was a glancing thud—but then we were through. The riders chased us for a while, but gave up about the time we turned on Atcheson. The ponies simply couldn't keep up.

After we'd lost them, and Bernie and I had calmed down a little, Bernie said, "So, aren't you a little old to be playing chicken?"

"Oh, you can't slow down," said Doughboy, sneaking a peek at us over his shoulder. "You do that, they smash the windows and drag you out."

"We lost two guys that way," said the Recruiting Poster.

Oh. Suddenly I was glad we had an escort.

Doughboy took us to the little video place, rousted out the owner, and we got what we needed. And twenty minutes after that, Officer Recruiting Poster (whose real name, I'd discovered, was Maynard, poor guy) escorted us into Chief Roderick's office. The chief was a big man, and a fat one, and when he rose from his desk to shake my hand I felt like the moon had come to pay a visit. He sat back down before the tidal forces overwhelmed me, and I hid a sigh of relief.

The Chief wasted no time on pleasantries. Instead, he leaned back in his tall leather chair and looked at me skeptically.

"Joe McGillicuddy vouches for you, Mr. Henderson, and Joe's word carries a lot of weight with me," he said, without a trace of irony. "When he called and said you'd like to see our guest and that I really ought to let you, I said, 'Why, sure, if you think it'll do some good.' But before I let you go in there, I'd like you to explain to me what you're hoping to accomplish."

Bernie began to bristle at his tone, but I jumped in before she could give him both barrels. It was nice to see her angry *for* me instead of angry *at* me, though.

"That's a fair question, Chief. I'm hoping to learn some things that will help us to send our friend and his fellow Mongols back home. And to do that, I need to talk to one of them."

"Hmph. It's a neat trick, if you can do it. But he doesn't

speak English, you know. He doesn't seem to speak Mongolian either, so far as we can tell. We had an expert down from the University, and he couldn't make heads or tails of it. Not that our guest has been all that chatty."

Bernie and I looked at each other. So maybe they weren't Mongols. Faux-Mongols? Ur-Mongols? Mingols! That was it. I'd call them Mingols.

"Not a talker, huh?" was all I said.

"No. Though if looks could kill, we'd be damn sight shorter of men around here."

"Well, Chief, I think I'll be able to talk with him; and I think I'll be able to get his attention. Give me a few hours, and I think maybe he'll be a lot more cooperative."

The Chief looked at me as though he'd just taken a bite of something foul tasting.

"I won't ask how you expect to do that. But you're not one of those jokers who thinks that if we just sit down and talk things out, all our problems will go away and everything will be sweetness and light, are you?" He made a waving motion with the fingers of both hands, like something flying away and vanishing.

He looked surprised and offended when I burst out laughing.

"Chief," I said at last, "I've never yet gotten away from a bully through sweet reason. At best I've only managed to baffle him long enough to find the fastest way to the door. But if our man's not a complete idiot, I've got some arguments here"—and I patted the bag I'd brought from the video place—"that I think he'll understand. With luck he'll find them persuasive."

The Chief looked unconvinced, but since I'd never known the cops to believe anything I said right off the bat I wasn't disturbed.

Finally, he said, "I'm sure you won't mind if I sit in."

"Of course not. The more the merrier. You might even enjoy it."

The Chief looked sour again, but finally he shrugged. "OK, then." He stood, warping the fabric of space in his vicinity, and gestured to Maynard the Recruiting Poster, who led us all down the hall.

"We've put him in the conference room," Maynard told us as we went. "We found out the hard way that our interview rooms are too small. You really don't want to be within arm's reach of him."

"He's violent?" asked Bernie.

"That too. But he stinks, and he's crawling with lice. We're probably going to have to have the conference room fumigated."

Bernie made a face. I did too, but on her it looked good.

The conference room was large and had all of the modern conveniences, even if the furniture was shabby and functional. Most particularly, there was a large flat-panel monitor at one end of the room, and a scowling Mingol in chains at the other. He was staring straight in front of him, and though his eyes went to us as we came in, they flicked back to wall almost immediately. His scowl deepened, though he didn't acknowledge our presence in any overt way. Then his eyes flicked back to me, just for a moment. Was that recognition? I wondered if I'd seen him careening down the aisle at Foodland, stretched out on the back of his pony. My skin crawled a bit, and Bernie's hand found mine. It felt cold.

I wanted to turn and run, but I forced myself to stand my ground. When you're small for your age, you learn never to let a bully know that you're afraid. To cover the awkward pause, I pretended to give him the once-over. He struck me as both fierce and well-used, like a tool that's still wicked sharp even if it's lost most of its paint and chrome plating. He had a long-healed scar on one side of his face, and a black eye on the other, and his nose had been broken a time or two. He had the air of one for whom being battered was a regular occurrence, unworthy of comment, and I decided then and there to call him "Sue".

I took a deep breath, which I regretted, and sat down at the other end of the table. That way I was not only facing Sue, I was directly beneath the monitor, which was exactly what I wanted.

And, of course, it put me as far away from him possible. And much closer to the exit. When you're small for your age you have to think about these things. And then the Chief sat down on my right, directly between me and the door. If I had to run, I'd have trouble scraping by him, darn him!

But you have to deal with things as they are, rather than things as you want them to be. So I thought better of taking another deep breath, and got on with it.

"Chief," I said, "could I possibly hook my laptop up to your monitor?" He nodded at Maynard, who demonstrated his ability to connect cables and turn on the TV. While I was attending to that, Bernie sat down on my left and touched me on the arm.

"Michael," she said. I glanced at her, and she motioned with her head toward our boy named Sue. I glanced his way, and saw why: instead of looking fierce, battered, and stoic, he now looked fierce, battered, and perplexed. Clearly, the finder was doing its job.

Perhaps it was time for a chat, before I started the show. I made myself grin at him.

"Sue," I began, "You seem to have been having a hard time."

He glared back at me, and I wondered how the device had translated "Sue". Then his eyes narrowed. "How is it that you know our speech? But it will not help you. My brothers shall slay you all like dogs!" His accent was thick and odd, but his speech was perfectly intelligible to me. Chief Roderick was looking at me as though I'd grown another head. I ignored him.

"Well, now, Sue," I said, "That's what I wanted to talk about. You see, it's more likely to be the other way around."

He barked a laugh. "Think you so? Your people are weak. Only a few of you can stand up to us, and your chief is soft and no warrior." He cast a contemptuous sneer on Chief Roderick.

"Bravado. Good for you." I smiled paternally at him. "But, you know, around here a leader's physique isn't nearly as important as the strength and determination of his men, and his skill at leading them." Chief Roderick stiffened, and then relaxed. Sue's sneer was unchanged. "Oh, I know what you're thinking, Sue, I really do," I said. "You're thinking that if we had any real warriors, you'd have faced them by now. You're thinking that you've got an open field here, and that nothing's going to stand in your way. You're thinking that there's nothing but raw meat and candy bars as far as the eye can see, and nothing to prevent you from taking them. Given what you've seen, that's understandable." I made myself lean forward. "The problem, Sue, is that you don't understand what's really going on here."

"That makes two of us," Bernie whispered in my ear. Sue turned his sneer back on me, but said nothing.

"That fellow with the red mustache," I said, and his gaze sharpened, "Yeah, you know the one. He sold you a bill of goods. He led you down the garden path. He brought you here like lambs to the slaughter, Sue."

I was trusting the finder to translate the idioms, and it appeared to be working, because he started growling again. I was getting to him.

"Cease to call me that word!" he shouted.

"Sue?" I asked. He looked murderously at me, and all the flesh of my body contracted like it was trying to hold tight to my bones. "You're not in a position to quibble," I said. I even managed to chuckle. Bravado, after all, runs both ways.

I thought Sue was going to take off for a moment, but he got a grip, and after a moment gave me an evil grin.

"You were not so quick to abuse me when last we met, Little Climber, though you were most quick in other ways." He grunted in derision. "Remove these chains and speak to me so."

I tilted my head to one side, and sighed wearily. "Sue, can you cut the tough guy act? We both know that if you got your hands on me you could break me in two like a twig. But let's face it, Sue." I waved a hand at myself. "It's no great skill. Lots of people can do it. Why, even Bernie here could do it if she tried."

Bernie raised an eyebrow at me.

"On the other hand," I continued, "lots of folks have tried it, but I'm still here."

Bernie leaned in. "Next time, for sure!" she whispered, in what I thought was an equivocal tone of voice. I smirked sidelong at her and continued.

"But you have a point, Sue. I'm sure you're a fine warrior and can ride down women and children with the best of them, so it's rude for me to insult you when you can't properly show your disapproval." I tented my hands, eyeing him; he just stared back down the table at me.

"Very well, then, Sue, what would you prefer to be called?"

Sue considered for a long moment; I suppose he was looking for the catch. At last, he spoke.

"I am called Sue," he said, with great force.

I blinked.

"Sue?" I asked. Had I heard him right?

"Sue," he repeated.

"Sue. Just...Sue."

"Yes."

"And that's better, is it?"

He nodded his assent.

"All right, then; Sue it is." I looked at him closely. He had crossed his arms across his chest—no mean feat, given the chains, and looked, if not happy, at least somewhat more gruntled than he had previously. I shook my head, and filed my puzzlement away for later.

"Well, anyway," I said, "Red Mustache led you astray. I don't know what he promised you, and I don't know what he was trying to accomplish, but it doesn't really matter. He's not going to deliver, because he's dead."

Sue twitched at that. The Chief looked from him to me and back again. Storm clouds were gathering on his brow, and I could almost hear him thinking, "There's a dead body you haven't told me about?"

Bernie leaned across the table to him.

"He brought the Romans here, too, and they killed him for it," she whispered. "The body's behind the Pancake Hut. We were all a little busy." He nodded slowly, and the clouds parted, revealing the face of the moon once again.

"Not that he was going pull it off," I continued, ignoring this bit of byplay. "You know what they say, Sue. Never start a vast project with half-vast ideas." Maynard, who was standing against the wall keeping an eye on our guest, choked down a laugh and then tried to look serious.

I opened my bag and rummaged through the selection of DVDs. "The trouble, Sue, is that you're assuming that these men here," and I waved at the Chief, Maynard, and the other officers in the room, "are our warriors. They aren't. Oh, they have weapons, and they know how to use them. But they aren't our fighting men.

"We do have warriors, Sue; and the reason you haven't seen them is that you're too picayune for them to bother with. Mopping you up would be a waste of their time. Attract their attention, though, and they'll slaughter you to the last man." I found the case I wanted, opened it, and slid the DVD into my laptop's optical drive. "Of course, you don't believe me. So I've organized a little film festival."

Sue's eyes widened as *The Longest Day* began to play on the monitor. I guess he'd never seen a TV before. Chief Roderick rolled his chair back to where he could see me, Sue, and the TV, and stared at me in astonishment. Bernie pulled her chair around so that she could watch the movie on my laptop's screen. I ignored them both; instead, I kept up a running narration for Sue's benefit.

"Sue," I said, "this is a movie about a war we fought about seventy years ago. We were attacked by enemies far nastier than you, and eventually it was time to take the war to them. Here's what happened." I skipped most of the slower parts, focussing on the scenes of death, destruction, and overwhelming force. Men dying on Omaha Beach; paratroopers descending on Sainte-Mère-Église and getting shot to pieces; landing craft frolicking in the surf. After about twenty minutes, Maynard went out and came back with several bags of microwave popcorn which he passed around.

Sue didn't get any, but it didn't matter; he was riveted.

When *The Longest Day* was over, Sue sneered at me some more.

"You think to frighten me, little climber," he said. "But though I know not what magic you used to produce these pictures, no warrior could be taken in by them. Real war is," and he showed his teeth, "more colorful."

I grinned right back, trying not to remember the slaughter at Foodland.

"Why, Sue, you're smarter than you look. You're right, of course. What you just saw was a recreation, like telling the story of a battle afterwards. After all, blood and screams are so unpleasant, aren't they?" And I inserted the disc of *Saving Private Ryan* into the laptop's optical drive and let it play. Sue's reaction was most gratifying.

After that, Maynard got me hooked up to the station's wireless network, and I trolled the 'net for interesting and pertinent videos. I showed him highlights from a number of History Channel documentaries. I showed him rifles. I showed him machine guns. I showed him tanks. I showed him ships. I showed him sudden, violent death by air, land, and sea. The last thing I showed him were some lovely shots of Hiroshima and Nagasaki, both before and after, as well as footage of a number of the nuclear tests in the Pacific. He'd seen enough explosions by then to have a good idea of what he was looking at.

Finally, I disconnected my laptop and put it away. Sue no longer looked contemptuous; I won't say he looked frightened, but he seemed very thoughtful indeed.

"Chief," I said, "Do you have a firing range in the building?"

The Chief had lost his look of astonishment an hour or so previous, and by this time he was grinning openly. "Why, yes, yes we do," he said.

"Seems likely to me that our friend Sue has probably never actually seen a gun fired in anger. Do you think your men could give him a demonstration? After that, we should give him some time to think. Is there any place the Mingols haven't shut down where Bernie and I can get a burger and fries?"

Four guards led Sue off to the range. Meanwhile, the Chief sent Maynard across the street to Hannity's Hamburger Hut, which had carefully been included in the barricade around the police station, and when he returned we settled down for lunch in the break room. The Chief had a triple bacon-cheeseburger; Bernie and I had singles. Bernie made a point of not ordering any french fries, and then stole mine without any trace of shame. When I called her on it, she just took another and chewed it at me.

My burger was good, anyway. I'd always avoided Hannity's, since its proximity to the police station meant that it was always full of guys in blue suits, but once this was all over I'd maybe add Hannity's to my weekly round. Well, at least until Dino's was rebuilt.

"I think I see what you're trying to do," said the Chief through a mouthful of beef and cheese. "Do you think it'll work?"

"That depends on our boy Sue," I said.

"He seemed rather subdued when we left," said Bernie.

"Oh, I think we've got him just where we want him," I said. "By this time it's got to be clear to him that his friends are going to be road pizza when the humvees get here. More than that, if these guys are anything like the real Mongols they'll have a firm grasp of military realities; if we can persuade them to make a strategic retreat, we're home free. The real question is how persuasive Sue can be, and whether whoever's in charge over in Corey Park will believe him."

Bernie nodded, but the Chief started visibly.

"Hold on, Mr. Henderson," he said when the moonquake had subsided. "Are you suggesting that we *release* this man?"

"Of course," I said. "There's no point in building a Trojan Horse if you don't wheel it up to the enemy gate. I need to talk to him some more, though."

"But he's a murderer! I can't just let him walk out of here!"

"No, sir," I said, "He's an enemy combatant and a prisoner of war."

"Think of him as an ambassador," said Bernie. "Diplomatic immunity and all that. Besides, it seems odd to worry about releasing one Mongol when there are hundreds of others roaming the streets, wild and free." She cocked a dark eyebrow at him as she stole my last french fry.

The Chief seemed inclined to argue, but I forestalled the discussion by wadding up my trash and tossing it in the bin.

"It's show time," I said.

Sue was deep in thought when we returned to the conference room, but he looked up as soon as we came in. No more Mr. Stoic, no sir.

"What do you want of me?" he said when we were all seated. "Why have you shown me these things?"

"It's important that you and your fellows have a clear understanding of your position here," I said. "We don't much like killing, but we can't allow you folks to keep doing what you're doing. It lowers property values. Best would be if you'd all toddle off home."

"Would that we could," he said. "But if the wizard is dead, as you say, then I do not know how we can." He looked bleak.

"We've seen your people appearing on some kind of platform in Corey Park. Was that the wizard's doing?"

"Yes." He shifted in his chair. "He brought me himself, but I know he planned to establish a bridge to this place."

"Can't you use this 'bridge' to get home?"

"No," he said. "I am not in our leader's confidence, but my cousin guards his tent. The wizard told the great Khazretgali that the magic worked one way only, but that he himself would bring our men home if need be." He made a motion that might have been a shrug. "And one had only to look at the bridge to see that it was damaged."

"So you've seen it, then."

"Yes. There were two halves, two platforms. One went all the way up," and he traced an arch in the air over his head with one hand, "but the other was broken off near the ground."

I nodded. "We have seen that half of the bridge. Khazretgali is your leader?"

"Yes. He united the clans to come to this place."

"Is he here? Or is he still at home—where you come from."

Sue seemed affronted. "He is here, of course. He led the first party across the bridge."

Interesting, I thought. So Khazretgali's deputy back home was still sending men through the gate; but since Red Mustache was dead the deputy could have no idea what was going on here.

"I might be able to get you home," I said. "It's possible. I know how Red Mustache brought you here. But first we need to stop the fighting."

"As you say."

I fished in my pocket and pulled out my lucky penny. I'd carried it since I was in second grade. I'd found it on the playground, and noticing that it had been minted the year of my birth I'd scratched my initials over the Lincoln Memorial with the point of a compass while Mrs. Martindale wasn't looking. Not that it had brought me all that much luck, but these things get to be a habit. I tossed it to him. I'm not sure why; I think I had a vague notion that maybe I could use it as an anchor if I needed to find Sue in a hurry.

"Keep that with you," I said. I glanced at Chief Roderick. He looked dyspeptic (as well he might after a triple bacon cheeseburger), but he didn't argue.

"Take our chum here out to the street and let him go," he told Maynard.

"Perhaps we'll meet again," I said, as Maynard and his partner escorted Sue to the door. Sue was looking stoic again, and pale.

"It is not likely, Little Climber," he said, and then he was gone.

Chapter 14

Once you've delivered the Trojan Horse, you have to wait for nightfall. There was nothing for us to do at the station, so Chief Roderick had Maynard and his cohorts take us back to my place.

Once we were moving, Bernie leaned forward and tapped on the metal grille.

"Maynard?" she said, "Could you go by my place first?"

"You're going home?" I asked. I was disappointed. I guess I was getting used to having her nearby.

"And miss out on all of this? You've got to be joking," she said. "But I need to get a few things."

"Oh," I said, and settled back into the seat. That was OK, then.

I didn't move when we got to Bernie's house. She stooped by the open car door, and looked in at me.

"Well, come on," she said. I looked back in surprise. She made that come-hither motion with her index finger. "Come on in. I want you to meet my mom." She had that tone in her voice —the one that's perfectly pleasant, but doesn't admit of contradiction.

I groaned, but crawled out of the car. What a day. I'd already faced policemen and pony-riding sociopaths; now I was going to have to face Bernie's parents. I was so far out of my comfort zone that I began to wonder whether I'd ever find my way back. Bernie had been there for all of it, which helped some...but honestly, Bernie was also a good bit of the problem. Still, though I wasn't entirely comfortable with Bernie I was glad she was along.

So then Bernie dropped me off in the kitchen with a quick, "Hi, Mom, this is Michael," and dashed upstairs.

Mrs. Balducci was a statuesque brunette; except for the hair, which was pulled back into a rather severe bun she looked a lot like an older Bernie. She was sitting at the kitchen table with a mug of coffee and a book of crossword puzzles.

"You've caught me being lazy," she said. "I ought to be out running errands today, but—" and she waved a hand out at the street and shrugged.

I smiled glassily. I think I managed a "Hi, Mrs. Balducci," but I'm not sure.

"So you're Bonnie Henderson's boy," she said. "I've seen you riding around town." She looked me up and down, mostly down, and then waved me to the seat across from her. "Your mom's right," she said. "We really need to do something about your wardrobe."

I think I blinked. I'm fairly sure that I looked puzzled. I was most definitely taken aback. What did my wardrobe have to do with anything? But that was quickly swallowed up by the realization that not only did she know my mom, they *talked* about me.

"You know my mother?"

She nodded. "We were in school together. And of course I've spoken with her on the phone several times recently."

I gulped, wondering what to say, and then felt a wave of relief when Bernie clattered back into the kitchen. It was short-lived, because Mrs. Balducci turned to her and said, "Don't you think Michael should do something about his wardrobe?"

Bernie got that look that people get when they agree with something someone's said about you but they don't want to hurt your feelings. You know, the raised shoulders, the eyes looking up and to the side (and away from *you*), and the head tilting side to side just a little.

"Well, yeah," she said.

You have to deal with the immediate threat. I put aside the notion that I was a topic of discussion for the mothers of Corey's End, and considered my options. I couldn't run. There was nowhere to hide. That left Plan C. I looked from Bernie to her mom and back again. "What's the matter with how I dress?" I asked, trying to stifle my indignation. I waved at my jeans and T-shirt. "I'm a programmer. This is how programmers dress."

Mrs. Balducci nodded. "Sure; but it's also how ten-year-old boys dress. In fact, I've seen any number of them wearing that exact same shirt."

I looked at Bernie for support. She looked embarrassed, but she nodded in confirmation.

I could feel myself turning red. "There was a sale," I said. "Can I help it if the only clothes Johansen's has in my size are in the kid's department?"

"There are other places to shop, you know," Mrs. Balducci said mildly.

"In this town?"

"There's this new thing they call the Internet," Bernie said, looking up at a corner of ceiling. "You might have heard about it."

"But don't sell Johansen's short, Michael. You're just looking in the wrong place," said Mrs. Balducci. "Get some cotton twill trousers, a nice belt, maybe a polo shirt or two or a button-down, you'd look ten years older, even from a distance." She glanced at Bernie. "Once this is all over, you should take him down there and help him find something, Bernie."

I shuddered. I wore the clothes I did because I could get in, grab them, and get out in a minimum of time. I had a sudden vision of Bernie helping me pick out clothes in the kid's section at Johansen's like a mom with her little boy, and taking an hour over it while everyone watched, including the Vikings. Oh, the embarrassment.

"Okay, okay," I said, just to make it stop. "I'll look into it. On-line," I added with a glance at Bernie, who had the grace to look relieved.

"We need to be going," she said. "We've got four police cars waiting outside."

"All right," said Mrs. Balducci, "I get the message." She gave Bernie a hard look. "Be good," she said, waving us out of the kitchen.

"Yes, Mom," said Bernie.

"Don't mind her," she went on as we walked to the car. "She's like that with everyone."

"Everyone?"

"Everyone that matters." She smiled.

"Oh. What's she like with people who don't matter?"

Bernie smirked.

"Oh," I said.

We reached my Mom's place without further incident, bar scattering a Mongol patrol or two. Bernie and I maintained our composures each time, but I can't say I enjoyed it. Maynard helped Bernie out of the back of the car; she responded by turning around and helping *me* out of the car. I tried not to smirk.

As we approached the front door, two of the four police cars drove off; the other two, including Maynard's, continued to clutter up the driveway.

"Aren't you going?" I asked.

"Nah," he said. "Since you're the only person we've got that can talk to those murderous bas—" and he glanced at Bernie, and continued, "—those Mongols, the Chief wants a 24-hour guard on you."

So Maynard the Recruiting Poster was going to be stuck sitting in the front yard? Better and better. Then I did smirk. Better outside than in.

"And you're on the first shift?" asked Bernie.

Maynard nodded glumly.

"Lucky you," she said. "I'll see if we can send out a thermos of coffee."

I stopped smirking, but I didn't growl. At least, I don't think I growled. But Bernie took me by the hand and led me inside, so that was OK.

We had a leisurely dinner with Mom, and then settled down to a game of Scrabble around the kitchen table. I did pretty well; in fact, I think I'd have won, except that Mom and Bernie wouldn't accept "SQL" as a valid Scrabble word. It was on a triple-word-score, too.

Through it all, we discussed what we'd learned and what we were going to do about it.

The first part was filling in Mom about our conversation with Sue. Bernie had a great time, and related the whole thing in four part harmony, with feeling. "But what was all that about the Mongol's name?" she asked me. "You seemed really puzzled by it."

"That's right—you were only privy to half the conversation," I said. "Well, the long and short of it was that he didn't like being called 'Sue'. So I asked him what he wanted to be called, and he told me to call him 'Sue'."

Bernie looked confused. "That can't be right," she said. "I don't remember exactly what he said, but he certainly never said anything like 'Sue'."

I looked at her blankly. "Huh? He said it repeatedly!"

"It's the finder," said Mom. "You have to remember, Bernie, that Michael didn't really hear anything the Mongol said. He just heard the finder's translation."

"OK, I get it," I said. "The finder's translation mechanism uses symbolic links to map between English words and the foreign equivalents. I'd named him 'Sue', and when the translator got a new foreign name for him it just updated the symbolic link to point at the new name."

Now Bernie looked really confused.

"He's always like this," said Mom. "Don't let it bother you."

"Sorry," I said. "Geek-speak. When Sue gave me his right name, the finder just corrected its translation, but kept the name 'Sue' as its English equivalent." I frowned. "Bernie, *you'd* better not call him 'Sue'."

"Trust me," she said, "I'd rather not call him anything."

After we'd rehashed the afternoon, Mom got us all some ice cream.

"So we know," I said when she returned, "that Red Mustache brought Sue and few others here himself, and then later set up a 'bridge' so that more could come over without his help. I wonder why he did that, and what was the point of bringing the Romans over as well?"

"At a guess," said Mom, "this Khazretgali fellow played him for a fool."

"How do you mean?"

"Well, think about it. You're a Traveler. You've got a finder all your own. You've got a living to make. What do you do with it?"

"Have adventures?"

"That's one, though it usually doesn't turn out well. What else?"

"Try to make it pay," said Bernie. I nodded, though I still had no idea how to do that.

"Bingo," said Mom. "There are lots of different ways to do that, of course—"

Oh, are there? I thought to myself.

"—but a common one is to set yourself up as a court wizard."

I waited a moment for Mom to go on, and then made the "get on with it" motion with my hand. Mom gave me a look.

"I see," said Bernie. "You try to find a patron who will support you in exchange for magical services rendered."

I pondered that.

"So what you're saying," I said slowly, "is that it isn't about *us* at all. When Red Mustache brought over the Vikings, for example, he was trying to ingratiate himself with *them*."

"Yup," said Mom. "Find some raiders, awe them with your powers, and offer to find them booty beyond their wildest dreams. Instant meal ticket, if you can deliver."

"It didn't work out all that well for him, though," I said, thinking of the Vikings at Johansen's Department Store. "They decided they didn't need him."

"By that time, they didn't," said Mom. "Your Red Mustache doesn't seem to have been all that bright."

"But if it's not about us, why did he keep following Michael around?" asked Bernie. "I mean, that's just weird."

"Yeah," I said, "How come he kept interrupting my lunch?"

"Perhaps he was trying to find lunch spots containing small, sarcastic software engineers," said Mom. I humphed. Her mouth quirked, and she went on, "But I suspect that it was probably due to finder bias."

This time it was Bernie who made the "get on with it" motion. At her, Mom chuckled.

"It's a term your father used. I guess some finders have a bias toward finding certain kinds of thing. If you don't allow for it, you get more than you bargained for."

Bernie grinned. "So maybe his finder has a bias for small sarcastic software engineers?"

I humphed at her.

"Well, no, probably not," said Mom. "But it might well have a bias for finding other Travelers. That, with his other requirements, may have been enough."

"So he was trying to find a modern, consumer-oriented culture like ours, with a ready source of fast food, and his finder added the condition that a Traveler be present?"

"Something like that."

I was struck by a thought. "Does that mean that those days when I didn't go out to lunch, he didn't appear here because the conditions weren't right?"

"It's a guess," said Mom.

"Well, but suppose he was trying anyway," I said. "What would happen?"

"Who knows? He might have ended up somewhere else, entirely. Or maybe he went nowhere. If a finder can't find what you're looking for, you just stay where you are."

"What about my father's finder?" I asked. I couldn't bring myself to call him "Dad". "Does it have a bias that I should know about?"

"Not that he ever said." Mom shrugged. "Sorry."

"But back to the Mongols," said Bernie. "You think he tried the wizard-thing with them, and then couldn't control them?"

"It seems likely," Mom said.

"And that explains the Romans!" I said, banging on the table. All of the Scrabble pieces jumped. "Whoops. Sorry. But that explains the Romans. It was damage control. He was looking for a fighting force that could contain the Mongols."

"It's a guess," repeated Mom. "Maybe he was just trying over again with a new force, and finder bias brought him back here."

"So much for past history," said Bernie. "But what do we do *now*?"

"Clean up the Scrabble board," said Mom. We both gave her a look at the same time. "First things first," she said.

"You were talking about anchors the other day," I said as I swept the tiles into the box. "Can I use someone else's anchor?"

"I'm not sure what you mean."

"Well, take Sue, for example. He must have relatives back on Nehwhon."

"Nehwhon?" asked Bernie, looking at me, eyebrows raised.

"Where the Mingols come from," said Mom.

Bernie turned the look on her. "Mingols?"

"Like Mongols," I said, "only different."

"Because they come from Nehwhon rather than here," Mom said.

Bernie tried to look at both of us at once.

"It's from an old fantasy series," I said, trying to face Bernie and shake my head slowly at my mom in disbelief all at the same time. Moms know the darndest things.

"Never mind," I went on. "Later. So Sue must have a mom or dad on Nehwhon. If he were a Traveler, he could use them as anchors, right?"

"Right," said Mom.

"Well, suppose I use my finder, and I take Sue with me. Can I use his mom or dad as an anchor? He's a particular person, and he only has one mother, and she lives in Nehwhon rather than anywhere else."

"It might work," she said doubtfully. "Your father never said anything about that."

"And then, the same thing should apply to the piece of bridge down in the park," said Bernie. "If it's got just one other end, then given that piece you ought to be able to find the other piece."

"Call 'em the bridge-head and the bridge-foot," I suggested. "It's a one-way trip, from head to foot."

"OK, so if you could get to the bridge-foot and find the bridge-head, you could take the foot with you."

"That would certainly prevent any more Mingols from coming across," I said. "But that still leaves the main problem. How do I get to the bridge-foot without getting skewered?" Actually, I was beginning to have an idea about that. But I didn't like it.

I waved that aside for later.

"One last thing, Mom. What are the odds that Red Mustache had a partner?"

She pursed her lips as she thought about it. "Unlikely," she said. "Travelers tend to avoid each other. Or so your father said."

"Got it."

And on that note we finished putting away the Scrabble game. Bernie and I talked for a while longer, and then I headed up to my apartment and went to bed. Of course, I had to stop on the way and give Maynard a thermos of coffee.

It took me quite a while to fall asleep after I crawled between the sheets—as you might guess, I had a lot on my mind. Most of it was completely practical: we had a nasty infestation of Mingols, and something had to be done about it, and it seemed that I was the one who had to do it.

I hate it when that happens.

So I lay there, staring at the ceiling I could dimly see in the light from my alarm clock, and pondered.

I'd spent the last six years living in my cave, interacting with customers over the 'net, and trying to keep other human contact to a minimum. Now here I was, thrust into the middle of things, with people depending on me, people I'd never been all that fond of. For them I was supposed to run the risk of being disemboweled by a Mingol spear while fleeing from Giant Hairy Man-Eating Locust Creatures with Dynamic Buzz-Saw Action?

And how was I supposed to get rid of the Mingols, anyway? Red Mustache had been able to bring small parties of men with him when he Traveled. I assumed that anything *he* could do I could do better, but still, lifting an entire park's worth of smelly little warriors was a bit of a stretch. And then there were their ponies, who contributed greatly to both the mass and the smell. Although, I suppose there was somebody in town who would be glad to take the ponies off of my hands if it came to that.

I couldn't help thinking of many of the fantasy novels I'd read, where the young kid born in difficult circumstances discovers that he has amazing, wonderful powers and proceeds to use them to kick serious butt while advancing the plot to a thrilling conclusion—all in a good cause, of course. *I* was born in difficult circumstances, or at least I'd grown up in them, and *I* had these new, amazing, wonderful powers; if I were the hero of one of those books, I'd use my powers to sneak into the park and send all of the Mingols to perdition in some suitably flashy and blood-thirsty manner. There'd be a cost, of course. I'd exceed my strength and collapse to the ground as the world seemed to end around me, pain filling my body, and finally I'd let the blackness take me and know nothing more. I might even wake up blind. But my friends would be with me when I woke up, and I'd get better, and everything would be grand, at least until the next time.

It was horribly appealing. There's always something appealing about just making the problem go away. Plague of Mingols? Just press the delete key, and they'll be gone! Yeah, there'll be massive spatters of blood, and moans, and bodies all over the place, but it's all on the computer screen, right? And when you're done playing, you quit the game, and the blood and death goes away, and you read your e-mail and then get back to work. Right? You don't even have to go blind.

Somehow, though, I didn't want to begin my career as a hero as some kind of glorified mass-murderer. The Mingols were stone killers, and they'd been practicing on my neighbors, but loathsome as they were they were still people. All I really wanted to do was send them home and prevent them from coming back. Let them find their own way to perdition, the dirty rotten stinkers.

The question was moot, of course, as I couldn't think of any practical way to use my newfound skills to slaughter the Mingols wholesale without joining them in death. If I *could* bring the whole kit and caboodle with me, I could jump with them into the middle of a lake, or an ocean, or a forest fire or an airless waste. And then, having exceeded my strength, light-headed with hunger and fatigue, I'd collapse to the ground (if there was any), pain filling my body, and let the blackness take me...and drown, or burn to death, or asphyxiate, and never see my mom or Bernie again.

Somehow I very much wanted to see Bernie again. In fact, dying without seeing Bernie again struck me as no way to live. And anyway, if I had to die the Mingols weren't the company I'd have chosen to venture into the Great Beyond with.

I'd like to point out, for those who might be wondering, that this sudden tenderness on my part for the lives of these pony-riding fiends had absolutely nothing to do with matters of size. Even if the Mingols were little guys right across the board (and they were), they were still too damn big. But I was learning that other people are people, too. If I had to kill some Mingols to defend my friends and family I'd do that. But I didn't want to Super Size it.

And maybe persons of size weren't so bad. Bernie was a person of size. And thinking of doing something great and stupid for Bernie—and for Joe and Brother Bear and Gaius Valens and Dino and my mom, too, but mostly for Bernie—I finally fell asleep.

For all of about fifteen minutes before I was roused by a solid knocking on my door.

When I opened the door, Maynard's big black flashlight was shining right in my face. I threw up my hand, squinting, and he pointed it further down with a grimace that I felt rather than saw.

"Michael," he said, "I need to take you down to the station. Something's come up." He didn't apologize for waking me...but the grim urgency in his voice was apology enough.

I didn't ask any questions. "I'll be right with you," I said. "Get Bernie, please. I'll need her."

"I don't think that's wise," he said, flatly.

"She's safest with me," I said. "And anyway, she'd kill me if I left her behind." Then I closed the door on that discussion, and got dressed. Moments later I joined Bernie in the back of the police cruiser.

"What's the deal?" asked Bernie.

Maynard's partner backed the cruiser out of Mom's driveway.

"Your friend Sue has come back," said Maynard. "Sort of." He didn't look back at us when he said it, and we didn't press him for details.

My hand found Bernie's, or hers found mine, and we rode the rest of the way in silence. It was after midnight. The streets were empty, and no lights were visible in the houses we passed. The street lights were off, too. The only illumination was our car's headlights and the green and red of the traffic signals at the major intersections. Even the bars and restaurants down on East Dunne were shuttered and dark.

We saw no other cars, and no signs of life until we turned onto Wilson Street and were passed through the barricade. The street lights were on outside the police station, and the windows of Hannity's Hamburger Hut were shockingly bright after the gloom filling the rest of the town. There were cops everywhere. Some were walking in and out of Hannity's with cups of coffee, but most were standing in a wide ring around a crumpled figure in the middle of the road.

Maynard's partner parked by the curb just short of the station. Chief Roderick met us as we climbed out of the cruiser. He looked tired and pale, and there were dark pouches under his eyes, and he was not smiling. He didn't say anything; he just inclined his head toward the body. We followed him in silence.

It was Sue, of course. He was dead, but he hadn't died easily. In fact, I was sure his killers had meant to make his death as difficult as possible for him. He was lying across the double yellow line, directly between Hannity's and the front door of the station. He'd been cut nearly to bits. From his neck down to his toes, no part of his body lacked the sign of the knife's passage. Only his face was untouched, presumably so we'd know who he was. It was hard to tell, but I rather thought he'd been beaten before they'd begun the slicing.

I didn't look for my lucky penny. They hadn't left him any place to keep it.

Bernie turned away. I put my arms around her waist, wishing I was taller, that I could be a tower of strength for her, even as I forced myself to look. This is what I'd been wishing on the Mingols, what, thank heavens, I'd turned away from.

There was surprisingly little blood. Evidently they'd killed him elsewhere, and then dumped his broken body here as a message.

In one of those books I was talking about, it would have said that his dead eyes stared at me reproachfully. They didn't, though. They just stared, the whites a pale orange in the sodium vapor of the street lights.

I felt the reproach anyway. I'd primed him, I'd programmed him like a guided missile, and sent him off to do my bidding, and like a guided missile he'd been destroyed. I remembered his last words to me. He had known it would happen. He'd gone anyway. A vicious killer, our Sue, but he had guts.

I swallowed, hard. All too plainly, he had guts.

"I guess he wasn't all that convincing," I said when at last I could speak. "Well, isn't this just ducky."

There really wasn't anything more to say. Men who would do

this to one of their own simply had to be stopped. And first, and most especially, I had to stop the influx of fresh troops. It might be beyond my strength, but I had to try. I wondered how I was going to get into the Mingol camp without Sue's help.

Bernie sobbed, and I held her as best I could, and eventually Maynard took us home.

Chapter 15

Some little time later, Mom and Bernie and I were sitting around Mom's kitchen table drinking cocoa. No one was talking. We'd filled her in on Sue's demise, and none of us felt like going to sleep with that rattling around in our brains. So we sat, and sipped, and stared at the table top. It was an odd table, and well-worth staring at, though of course growing up I hadn't seen anything odd about it. It was green, as I've noted before, and intricately carved. It had a Chinese look to me, but that might only be because it was made of something that looked and felt very like a darkish kind of jade. It couldn't really have been jade, though. Jade's pretty soft, and I'd banged on this one often enough to know that it was impervious to harm. I wondered if my father had brought it home to Mom from some other world-line. Anyway, the top was smooth, and veined with darker and lighter shades of green, and an apparent depth that drew the eyes, especially when, as now, the attached brain wasn't much inclined to think.

A knocking on the door interrupted my musings, such as they were. We all looked at each other, and with a collective sigh we trooped out to the front room. When we got there I looked at Mom, and she looked right back at me, unmoving, and so I opened the door.

It was Maynard, of course. Proving that Maynard *can* be taught, his big black flashlight was pointed politely at the bricks of the front step, rather than in my face.

"What now?" I asked. I expect my tone implied that it had better be good. I suppose I should have been more polite; I'd been inside drinking cocoa while Maynard had been out in the cold guarding us from harm.

Maynard just stepped to one side and gestured toward the driveway.

Immediately behind him were the two police cruisers. You know how police cars have those spotlights mounted on the front? Both of them were turned on, and both were shining down the driveway toward the street. And caught right in the middle of the driveway, right in the intersection of the two beams with two black, black shadows stretching out behind him, a Mingol sat his pony, stoically bearing the brightness of the spot light. His pony raised its head and whickered; he himself might have been made of the same stone as my Mom's table, except that of course he wasn't green. His hands held only the reins. Twenty or thirty feet behind him, actually out in the street, I could dimly make out two other riders

The one on the driveway was bigger than the other Mingols I'd seen, and clad in the same dirty skins and furry hat. But I thought he was older than most, and unlike the others his skins were studded with small white objects that shone in the spotlight. With a shudder I guessed that they might be human teeth. I almost dubbed him Tooth-Bearer then and there, but remembering how my finder had translated Sue's real name as "Sue" I thought better of it. Better I found out what he was really called.

I stepped out of the house and up to Maynard's cruiser, where I could see the Mingol easily enough, but he'd have trouble getting at me, especially if I ducked. The hood of the cruiser was cold under my hands. Maynard crouched down to my right.

"He rode up a couple of minutes ago."

"Has he said anything?"

"No. He just sits there."

And the Mingol just continued to sit there, unmoving. After a few moments I realized that he couldn't see us in the glare from the spot lights. That meant the ball was in our court. Pity. I was always lousy at basketball.

"What do you want?" I called out, settling for the direct approach.

He raised his chin slightly. "I would speak with the little climber."

Well, naturally, I thought. Why else would he be here at this hour? It disturbed me, rather. The Mingols knew who I was and where I lived. That was an outcome I hadn't expected, and it struck me as a Bad Thing. I wondered how they had found me.

"Who wants him?" I called back.

"I am called Tooth-Bearer. The one called Sue belonged to my clan."

Great. "Tooth-Bearer." Apparently giving nicknames to strangers was one habit I was just going to have to try to break.

"And what do you want of him?" I could hear Bernie moving impatiently behind me, and remembered that she and the others could only understand half of the conversation. I resolved to try to make my half carry as much freight as possible. "What does Tooth-Bearer want of the Little Climber?"

"Vengeance. My clansman is dead."

Better and better. Now the Mingols had a personal vendetta against me in particular. That begged the question, though: why hadn't they come in force? But wait.... Sue had been killed by the Mingols, not by our guys. Why would they seek to revenge his death at my house? Was there division in the Mingol camp? I decided to play dumb.

"Your cousin was my enemy," I called back. "But I did not intend his death. Why do you seek vengeance against me?"

"My cousin was killed by the great Khazretgali. It is against him that I require vengeance."

That stopped me.

"You want *my* help in killing Khazretgali? I don't see how I can help with that."

Tooth-Bearer snorted, the first sign of emotion I'd seen from him. "Khazretgali will die," he said. "I shall kill him myself. His purposes shall be frustrated, and his deeds shall be forgotten. He shall not see tomorrow's sunset." The words were harsh, solid, final, and I was glad they were not directed at me.

I leaned over toward Maynard. "Could your guys point their spotlights a little more toward the ground? Our visitor doesn't seem disposed to attack us, so there's no need to blind him." I spoke quietly, but still chose my words with care—there was no knowing how acute Tooth-Bearer's hearing was.

"Are you sure? These guys are awfully fast; right now, keeping the light in his eyes may be our best defense."

"I know, but I think we have to show willing. Besides, you guys are armed."

"Fat lot of good that'll do you if he aims for you first."

"Just do it, will you?"

"It's your funeral. I hope it isn't mine, too," he said. "Parsons! Jackson! Lower the beams a bit."

There was few moment's delay, and then first one beam and then the other came down until they were shining at the pony rather than its rider. The pony tossed its head and made as if to turn around, but Tooth-Bearer settled it with a jerk on the reins.

"If you plan to take care of Khazretgali yourself," I called out, "and I've no doubt you can, what help do you need from me?"

"My clansman came to me with a strange tale. He told me of weapons of great power, and of the death of thousands. I, Tooth-Bearer, chief of his clan, I myself escorted him into Khazretgali's presence and told him to speak. He began to describe what he had heard and seen. Long before he had told the full tale the great Khazretgali cursed him, calling him a traitor and a coward, and sentenced him to die a coward's death." The scowl on Tooth-Bearer's face was a fearsome thing. "Chief of chiefs is Khazretgali, but my clansmen are mine to punish and mine to reward. He has dishonored my clan. He has disgraced his position. He is a fool." The contempt in Tooth-Bearer's voice cut like a knife.

"A wise leader does not kill the bearer of bad news," I agreed. "We call that 'shooting the messenger.' But I still do not know what you want of me."

"I shall kill Khazretgali. I shall frustrate his plans. But first I must know—did my clansman speak truth? Did he judge correctly? I wish you to show me what you showed him. And then, when Khazretgali is dead, you shall bring us home."

Frustrate his plans... I had to fight down a rising sense of exaltation. I'd had some ideas of how to send the Mingols packing, but they'd gone down in flames when Sue turned up dead. Now it began to look like we were back in business. If only....

"Tell me," I called. "Did Sue speak of me to the great Khazretgali? Did he describe the Little Climber? Did he speak of returning to your home?"

"He did not," said Tooth-Bearer, "for I directed him not to. Well I knew how Khazretgali would respond to his words. He is a fool, a man of arrogance and vanity. Sue knew as well. He died nobly, that Khazretgali's unfitness to lead the clans might be made manifest."

"How did Khazretgail come to lead the clans to begin with?"

"He had the aid of the mustached one. But you say that one is dead."

"I have seen his body," I said.

I felt a chill. Tooth-Bearer had sent Sue, his own clansman, to his death so as to win at the game of inter-clan politics. Perhaps we could work with him, but I resolved to keep my long spoon handy. At the same time that feeling of exaltation came back full force. It was like the moment when a complex software design comes together, all the pieces dropping neatly into place. Red Mustache was the foundation of Mingol power in Corey's End; and Red Mustache was dead. That was the wedge that would strike at the heart of his alliance of clans and make it all fall down go boom—and Khazretgali didn't know it. And if Khazretgali was not aware of me or my appearance, my plan could still work.

"I can show you what I showed your cousin," I said. "I can do more than that, if you will help." I thought I heard a stifled gasp from Bernie; or maybe it was from my Mom.

Tooth-Bearer made no response, but gazed at me steadily. I didn't think he could actually see me through the glare, but he clearly had a good sense of where my voice was coming from.

"But how do I know that *you* speak the truth?" I asked. "How do I know that Sue was truly your man?"

Tooth-Bearer said nothing, but simply raised one hand, opening it to show something held between his thumb and forefinger, something that glinted in the spotlights.

My lucky penny.

"Maynard, kill the spotlights," I said. "We have much to speak of with this man."

Things moved quickly after our late night/early morning parley with Tooth-Bearer and his men, and noon found me, as by the workings of a well-oiled machine, tied firmly to a tree in the approximate center of Corey Park.

This was Not According To The Plan, mind you, and I was somewhat broken up about it.

I don't know what kind of tree it was; trees have never really been on my radar except as things not to run my bike into. The trunk of this tree was bigger around than I am, and rough, and bumpy. There was one large bump right under my left shoulder blade that should have burst into flame from the hate I directed at it. The trunk tilted back at an angle that might look restful from a distance but meant that my body kept trying to slide down and away from the tree, which put pressure on my feet, and also on my shins where the rope ran across them. My arms were stretched back behind me on either side of the trunk with my wrists joined by another length of rope, which meant that I couldn't even push myself up with my hands. And on top of the aches in my feet and my ankles and my shoulders and my left shoulder blade, there were ants running up and down the tree and using me as a ladder, itching and tickling.

And then, all around me was the Mingol camp. Don't get me started about the smell of the camp.

But it was shady, and I had a good view. The Great Khazretgali had had me tied about ten yards away from the bridge platform and directly facing it. The platform's metalwork wasn't identical to anything Bernie and I had seen in the Old City, but it had the same flavor, the same twisted, semi-organic shapes, the same many-sided and star-shaped openings. Every few minutes another Mingol appeared on it, pony and all, to be greeted by several of Khazretgali's officers. I have to say, they were no slouches at crowd control—each new arrival was hustled away to another part of the park, there to join his fellows.

Each time a Mingol appeared, the bridge platform emitted a blue pulse as from thousands of tiny markings, confirmation, if I'd needed it, that the bridge was akin to the finders.

Mom hadn't been pleased by my plan. She'd sat, tight-lipped, as we'd worked out the details with Tooth-Bearer around the old picnic table on the back porch The arms, they were not crossed. The foot, it was not tapping. But the Mom, she was not happy. When the Mingol and his men had gone, I turned to her.

"I think we've got it," I said. "What do you think, Mom?"

She looked down. She seemed smaller than I'd remembered, drawn in on herself. Her hands were folded in her lap. "Don't do this, Michael," she said in a low voice.

I grimaced. "I don't like it either, Mom. But what else can I do?" I ran through the options. "Plan A doesn't work. I mean, I can run away easily enough. Hell, I can run away easier than anyone else on the planet, now that Red Mustache is dead. But I can't take all of you with me. I could take you, and Bernie, and maybe a few others, but I can't take Joe or Brother Bear, or even the insufferable Maynard. And they wouldn't go if I offered. This town is their home, and it's my home too.

"Plan B is out for the same reason. And that leaves Plan C, and I'm the only guy in town that may be able to send the Mingols back home."

Mom was still looking down at the green complexity of the

table top, though I don't think she was actually seeing it.

"Mom, look at me. Please."

Slowly she raised her head, and I flinched at the fear in her eyes. It was too much like the fear in the pit of my stomach. Bernie, who was sitting to my right, put her hand on my arm. I was glad for it. Saving the world was so not my thing. I hadn't been trained for it. I had, in fact, been trained to save myself and let everybody else go hang. But I had discovered that there *were* good people in my town, that I actually liked them, that my size wasn't necessarily the bar to normal human friendships I had always thought it was. I owed all that to Bernie...and I'd need every bit of her fire and her conviction to get through this.

"Mom," I said, "I hate it. I don't want to do it. I want to go upstairs and pull the covers over my head. But I don't get to do that anymore. I have to try, Mom."

"Don't do it, Michael," she whispered. "Run away. Run away."

It was my turn to look away. "Please, Mom, don't. It's hard enough for me as it is." She stood up, and a few moments later I heard the door to the back hallway open and close.

I groaned at the memory, as the bridge pulsed and another Mingol appeared. That had been our last conversation. I went looking for her before I left, but she had shut herself up in her bedroom, and refused to speak with me. And she had been right. What good had I done, getting myself tied up like this? I couldn't run, I couldn't hide, and I couldn't take direct action against the enemy. I cursed myself for not having developed a Plan D: what to do if captured. But, of course, Plans A, B and C were all about *not* getting captured. Even Plan C was only about gaining time until you could execute either Plan A or Plan B.

For about the five-hundredth time I tried to shift my body to avoid the bump under my shoulder blade. It just made my arms and shins and back ache more.

But then, what would Plan D have looked like? When you've been captured, your freedom of choice is rather limited.

I looked across the park. I could see parts of the low concrete wall that separated the park from the sidewalk, and glimpses of buildings beyond that. I couldn't see Mary Claire's apartment, but I knew it was up there, blocked from my view by the overhanging branches of the tree I was coming to hate with every bone, muscle, and sinew in my body. Joe was up there, and Brother Bear, and Gaius Valens. And Bernie was up there.

Plan D. My lips curled sourly. Plan D, wait to be rescued.

Midmorning had found me riding into Corey Park on the back of a borrowed Mingol pony, with an honor guard of Mingol warriors. Tooth-Bearer's men, of course. I'd left Bernie with Maynard and his partner at Mary Claire's apartment, where Joe and Brother Bear were still keeping watch. I'd hated to do it, Maynard being Maynard, but I figured that Joe would keep an eye on him for me, and keep him from making any false moves where Bernie was concerned. Though possibly Gaius Valens was the bigger threat—he had seemed very glad to see her. But Bernie had given me a big hug when I left, so I wasn't *too* worried.

I was especially glad of that hug after I'd mounted the pony that Tooth-Bearer's men had brought for me. Not only was I riding into danger, a deeply unnatural act, I felt like a little kid. I'd last been on a pony when I was about six years old, on a trip to the county fair, and the feel of the saddle and the movement of the pony took me right back. Bernie's choice of clothing for my daring mission didn't help any.

When I was eleven, and just beginning to be small for my age, my mom signed me up for taekwondo lessons. I guess she thought that skill at a martial art would be good for my self-confidence, but it didn't go well. I had a bad attitude about it — what, you want me to stand there and let him try to *hit* me? Are you nuts?—which did not improve over the year that I was engaged in it, and on top of that I got steadily smaller for my age as the year went on. The one positive thing I had taken away from those days of pain and humiliation was my taekwondo suit. Getting hit by bigger kids was lousy, but getting to dress like Luke Skywalker, now that was *cool*.

I grew out of that, if "grew" is the right word for someone who remained the same size as he got older, and the suit had migrated to the back of my bottom-right dresser drawer, where it stayed. If I'd been a normal kid I suppose Mom would have gotten rid of it when I grew out of it, along with all of the too-small trousers and T-shirts, but after my tenth birthday I never actually grew out of anything.

Which is not to say that the suit fit all that well. I'd filled out a bit over the last ten years, and the white trousers were too snug for comfort as I shifted uneasily in the saddle. At least this was their last hurrah. Given the vermin I expected to encounter in the Mingol camp—that I was already encountering on the Mingol pony—I rather thought I'd prefer to drop the entire outfit in a dumpster somewhere than wear it back into my apartment.

The Skywalker suit had been Bernie's idea. Not this particular outfit, which naturally she'd been unaware of, but she'd argued that I couldn't wear my regular clothes.

"You're not supposed to be from here," she said. "That's going to be a hard sell if you're dressed like everyone Khazretgali's seen in town. You need to wear something exotic."

"Exotic? I don't have anything exotic," I'd protested. And she'd burrowed right into my closet and my dresser drawers until she emerged, victorious, with my taekwondo suit. It had yellowed, and there was a small tear on one knee (the fruit of a bold offensive against the Empire), but it was the best we could do.

Despite the apparent simplicity of my attire, I was not unequipped. I had a hunter's knife in a sheath on my belt, a gift from Brother Bear. I wore it as a piece of misdirection: if things went south and they took me captive, perhaps the presence of an obvious weapon openly worn would distract them from looking for hidden weapons. Plus, I had a notion that the Mingols would take me more seriously if I was armed.

Under the belted jacket I wore a baggy black T-shirt, Bernie's one concession to my personal comfort, and under that my finder's shoulder holster. Bernie had cut a small hole in the armpit of the T-shirt so that I could activate the finder without being obvious about it. Granted, I'd look like I was scratching myself, but the Mingols shouldn't think that anything out of the ordinary. The T-shirt also covered my food supply, an even dozen high-protein energy bars strapped to my abdomen with ace bandages. I wasn't sure how much Traveling I'd need to do, and pepper crackers and merchant oil don't grow on trees—or, at least, not on the trees in Corey Park. (And if they did, the ants would probably have gobbled them up.) I had a few other surprises secreted about my person. I wasn't taking any chances. Or, rather, I was taking far too many, and I wanted to even the odds by any means possible.

And so there I was, feeling like a little boy on a pony ride, dressed like Luke Skywalker at his whiniest, scared half out of my wits, surrounded by smelly, vermin-infested warriors who would kill me as soon as look at me if Tooth-Bearer gave the word, riding on a smelly, vermin-infested pony into the midst of a much larger group of warriors who would as soon kill me whether Tooth-Bearer gave the word or not, breathing shallowly because of the stench and the ace bandages wrapped around my middle. I had to make a conscious effort not to finger the finder in my left armpit. I longed to push the button and disappear.

The only thing that kept me going was the warmth of Bernie's parting hug, and the pride in her eyes, and the ready encouragement of Joe and the others. That and the memory of the terror on Bernie's face the day I'd first seen her, the day the Mingols came to Foodland and she'd taken refuge behind the manager's desk. That, and the thought of what might have happened to her if she'd been just a few feet further away from it when the Mingols had burst into the store.

Joe and Brother Bear thought I could do this. Bernie thought I could do this. I wasn't so sure. But I didn't want to let them down.

As we entered the park I found myself thinking, *Into the valley of death rode the six hundred.* It was not a comforting thought.

Chapter 16

Bernie had originally wanted to send a Roman bodyguard into the park with me, to protect me and keep me safe. Gaius Valens had agreed, and his words about stinking barbarians were both memorable and entertaining—even Brother Bear was impressed, and he doesn't speak Latin. But I'd reluctantly had to nix the idea.

First of all, I was trying not to get killed. Far from making me safer, approaching Corey Park with an armed guard was an invitation to violence. The Mingols had hated the Romans at first sight, and if any of them came with me I rather thought that the arrows would start to fly before I got close enough to do any good. Instead, my best chance of success was to be bold and fearless—to act, indeed, as if I had every right to be there, and as one with no reason for fear. The Mingols would take advantage of that, doubtless, but I had to hope that they'd respect it.

There was also Tooth-Bearer to consider. He had every reason to keep me on a short leash, and he wouldn't have gone for a Roman bodyguard at all, at all. Or, rather, he would have gone for them immediately, and I might have died in the ensuing fracas without ever leaving the street in front of Mary Claire's apartment. Alas, he had no reason to trust me, and I perforce had to trust him.

And so, throughout the pony ride I'd done my best to project an air of stern power and dignity, of boldness and steely resolve...all while looking like a ten-year-old Star Wars fan. It was an uphill battle, and at intervals I wondered why I hadn't had the sense to identify with Han Solo rather than Luke Skywalker. Han was one bad dude, and if I got into trouble I could always shoot first.

But that was only at intervals. Mostly, behind my mask of boldness and resolve (to the extent that I actually had one, which I don't know because I didn't bring a mirror, and the Mingols weren't telling) I was consumed by thoughts of fear and politics.

I'd asked Tooth-Bearer why, if he was going to kill Khazretgali anyway, he didn't simply do the deed and take over himself? And the answer, boiled down and reduced like a fine sauce, was, simply, "It's complicated."

It turned out that the assembled Mingols weren't all from one clan or tribe. There were four major chiefs, Tooth-Bearer among them, and a number of minor ones. Khazretgali was the Great Chief, the Chief of Chiefs, a position he'd acquired by offering to bring the other clans along on his invasion. Until then, he'd been strictly a minor league chief, the kind that the other chiefs bullied and laughed about behind his back when they didn't ignore him completely.

And the invasion, of course, was due to the abilities of Khazretgali's red-mustached shaman—and everyone knew it. The first two Mingol raids had been sales trips, in which Khazretgali had revealed his powers and the wealth of our town to a select set of warriors hand-picked by the four major chiefs. The grand invasion had followed.

And now Red Mustache was dead...and of all the Mingols, only Tooth-Bearer and his men knew it. And with that simple fact, Khazretgali's days were numbered. The Mingols firmly believed in the principle of "What have you done for me lately?" Once the death of Khazretgali's shaman became known, once it was clear that Khazretgali no longer had any special role to play in delivering the goods, he'd go back to being an object of scorn and derision—and the alliance of clans would collapse.

We caused quite a stir as we crossed the street and passed

through the stone pillars that marked the entrance to Corey Park, my Mingol honor guard and I (I frantically projecting dignity and resolve with every ounce of my being). Tooth-Bearer had explained to me that Mingols didn't take prisoners; they were too much trouble. Sudden death was easier, and had fewer complications, and hey, look at all these lovely teeth! So who was I, and why was a scouting party bringing me into camp? Heads turned toward us from all corners of the park, and a small knot of men began to move toward us from that spot in the center where I knew the bridge platform to be.

As they drew closer it was easy to figure out which one was Khazretgali. He was no bigger than the others, and he was dressed in the same kind of furs, but he had even more teeth sewn on his coat than Tooth-Bearer did, and I could swear that the shoulders were padded to make him look more imposing. Pathetic, that. They say that clothes make the man, but I'm here to tell you, they can't make him any bigger than he is. His fur hat was also sewn with teeth, and had a golden figure of an eagle stuck on top that wobbled back and forth with each of Khazretgali's swaggering steps. There was something about that eagle, something familiar, something that reminded me of my school days. Had I seen a picture of such a thing in a history book? And where did he get such a gaudy thing as that? He'd been a minor chief just days earlier...and surely the other chiefs hadn't given it to him.

And then it clicked—I knew what it was, and where it had come from. I remembered sitting on a bench in the school cafetorium, looking up at the stage. There were two flags, one on either side of the stage, and the one on the left, the American flag, had an eagle just like that at the top of its staff. Gaudy, yes, and no doubt impressive as all get out to a barbarian from a place so far out in the sticks that you literally couldn't get there from here, but easily come by.

Easily come by, that is, if you could just bop down to Johansen's Department store or some such place, buy a flag and flag staff and a cheap hacksaw, and chop the eagle off of the top.

I could just picture Red Mustache meeting with Khazretgali, flattering him, telling him that he deserved better, that he should be the Chief of Chiefs...and that with a little help, it all could be in his grasp. There's this place, see, Khaz, where the streets are lined with gold. Imagine your power if you were to lead the Mingol hordes to plunder and victory, wealth beyond the dreams of your people. Ahhhh, you doubt me? Here, take this. Keep it as a sign of your rule over all of the tribes. And there is more where this came from....

And of course Khazretgali had fallen for it.

I had him, now. That little mass-produced eagle bobbing on the top of his head showed me what kind of man he was. Khazretgali was what they call a parvenu, a nouveau riche. He had to be seen to be better than all others, because he knew they were better than he. So if Tooth-Bearer had teeth on his coat, Khazretgali would have even more teeth. And not on his coat, only, but on his hat, too! And then, to add to that a kitschy gold American eagle. It was too much. Despite my fears, I almost laughed in his face. I might be small outside, but Khaz was small inside.

I restrained myself, though. After all, it was show time, and after all, Khazretgali's lack of taste made him no less deadly.

My honor guard all dismounted as Khazretgali and the other chiefs drew near. I did not. Tooth-Bearer was with them, standing to Khazretgali's left. He regarded me impassively. He gave no sign of recognition, which was as we had agreed.

Khazretgali stepped out from the midst of them, arms akimbo, and looked me up and down, sneering. "What living carrion is this?" he said. "Why is it not dead? Kill it, and bring its teeth to me."

Boldness and resolve, I thought. Resolve and boldness. And scorn. Definitely scorn.

"Be wary, O Khazretgali," I said. "A shaman makes a powerful enemy."

Khazretgali grunted a laugh, looking round at those to his right and his left, as if inviting them to share the joke. The eagle bobbed on his head. "You, a shaman? Do they now acquaint little boys with the sacred mysteries?"

"Things are not always as they seem, O Great Khazretgali," I retorted, accenting the word "Great" with as much disdain as I could muster. "What have you done with my colleague, he of the Red Mustache?"

Khazretgali's face tightened with anger. Like most little men, he didn't like being challenged.

"He is about my business, Little Climber," he said, and I froze. And in that moment, Khazretgali gestured to his men. "Take him," he said. "And bind his mouth. He is no shaman, and his speech wearies me. Still, he might be useful." And I saw Tooth-Bearer nod, and my erstwhile bodyguard did that thing with efficiency and dispatch. And moments later I made the acquaintance of my nemesis the Bumpy Tree. I'd like to say that I put up a fight, but I didn't. Fights are dangerous. People get killed in them.

Presenting myself as a shaman, the colleague of Red Mustache, had been Tooth-Bearer's idea.

"Why not just tell everyone that Red Mustache is dead?" I'd asked. "Tell everyone that Khazretgali's source of power is gone, and undermine his authority. Then you can kill him and seize control."

Tooth-Bearer grunted in derision.

"You forget the other chiefs, Little Climber. Without Khazretgali and his shaman, our clans have no unity. We would fight, and who would win? Possibly Tooth-Bearer; possibly some other." He raised a hand, and gestured at my mother's house, at the acres of suburbia around us, and by extension at the whole town. "I do not like this place. The black stone is harsh under our hooves, and your works block out the sky.

"To raid your people is glorious. To become them is less so. Living here we would become soft, and forget the wide lands of our ancestors. But Tooth-Bearer cannot lead his people home if Tooth-Bearer is dead."

And that was the crux of the matter. Our interests ran

together: I wanted to send the Mingols home with a minimum of bloodshed, and Tooth-Bearer wanted to lead them there. To do that, Tooth-Bearer needed to be Great Chief. And the only certain way to supplant Khaz was to acquire his own shaman, his own source of power.

Which is to say, little old me.

Still, it had seemed reasonable at the time; after all, I had every bit as much claim to be called a shaman as Red Mustache did.

But we had miscalculated, Tooth-Bearer and I, and that doubly. First, our scheme presumed that I could plausibly present myself as a compatriot of the late, unlamented Red Mustache, Khazretgali not knowing me from Adam. But apparently Khaz had led those initial raids himself, and apparently my antics at Foodland and #1 Market had gotten more attention than I'd realized. And second, I'd forgotten to consider what Red Mustache was doing with a century of Roman soldiers. We'd even conjectured, Bernie and I, that maybe he'd found the Mingols too much to handle and had gone looking for help...or maybe had simply planned to try again with another group.

And that meant that Khazretgali knew that Red Mustache was gone for good—and didn't care. Maybe he thought that his position was strong enough without magical support. And perhaps it was. Khazretgali had promised to lead the clans on an invasion of a great and glorious and wealthy land, where the streets were lined with gold, and he had delivered. Granted, without Red Mustache the clans couldn't return home. But why would Khaz want to return home, home where he was a nobody? He had already delivered the goods. All he needed, now, was time to consolidate his rule. And for that, an absent shaman "about my business" might be as good as a visible one, and considerably less trouble.

If we could prove that Red Mustache was dead, the whole house of cards might come falling down. But we didn't have the body handy, and though Tooth-Bearer could claim that Red

Mustache was dead, it would be his word against Khazretgali's.

I made a mental note: if you take direct action against the enemy when you don't have to, make very sure you can bring it off.

Meanwhile, here I was, tied to a tree, waiting on Khazretgali's pleasure.

What fun.

The Mingols left me pretty much alone after they tied me to the tree, which surprised me—I was expecting a little of what the books call "rude sport" and Mrs. Henderson's son Michael calls "middle school."   Instead, the riders gave me a wide berth, though I collected an unpleasant glance now and then. I guess it was because Khazretgali had claimed me...and a Mingol warrior didn't touch that which was Khazretgali's, not if he wanted to die in battle. Even Khazretgali ignored me, once I was tied, though I did notice him staring at me once. He caught my glance, and gave me an evil smirk that raised goose bumps all over my body. Then he turned and barked some orders I couldn't quite hear. I watched with some concern—that's called understatement, if you're unfamiliar with it—but all that happened is that Khazretgali mounted and rode off with several squads of men. I felt a sudden stab of fear for my Mom; I was glad there were still a couple of squad cars watching the house.

I spent the first twenty minutes or so of my captivity cursing Tooth-Bearer up one side and down the other for not standing by me when Khazretgali had me taken captive. Silently, of course. There's nothing more foolish-looking than a person who's small for his age swearing a blue streak, especially when it's directed at a fellow rather taller than he is. I'd learned this to my cost in middle school, and Joey Swenson had called me Gonzo the Performing Monkey for years after.   I never tried that again. True, a teacher had heard me, and told the vice-principal (she'd been both impressed and appalled by the depth and range of my fulminations), and the vice-principal had threatened to call my mom.   That was a possibility too dire for words, but it was unneeded; I had already learned my lesson. I *hate* looking foolish.

Eventually I wound down, the way you do, and started thinking. And after quite a lot of that, including the various thoughts and reminiscences I've already described, the penny dropped, and I started cursing Tooth-Bearer all over again.

He'd expected this. That's why he hadn't done anything when Khazretgali took me captive. No, worse, he'd *planned* this, the smelly, stinking...words failed me.

Of course I'd been taken captive. I'd challenged Khazretgali's authority; of course he'd responded badly. Why had I expected anything else? And that meant that Tooth-Bearer had planned for me to get tied up like this, if not worse. Was this a betrayal?

It took me a few more minutes, but I puzzled it out in the end. Tooth-Bearer needed me—but he had to show that I could be controlled. A shaman that can't be controlled is a danger, but a shaman under your thumb is an asset. If he wanted to dominate the tribes with my help, he had to show that he was in charge, not me. And then, there was the tactical effect. I'd been brought in by Tooth-Bearer's own men. By not defending me, he had distanced himself from me. No one, least of all Khazretgali, would think that Tooth-Bearer and I were working together.

And all that meant that Tooth-Bearer would arrange to have me freed in his own good time. I hoped he wouldn't take too long. That bump under my shoulder blade had me about ready to scream, except that I couldn't scream because I'd been gagged, and my sinuses were beginning to close up because of the pollen from the trees and grass, and I couldn't reach my finder because my arms were tied behind me, or Red Mustache's finder either. But mostly I was worried about Joe and Brother Bear and company. They had to have seen the Mingols grab me, and if they sent the Romans in to rescue me before Tooth-Bearer made his move, Things Would Not End Well.

You wouldn't think that being tied to a tree would be so conducive to rational thought. But needs must when the Devil drives; and also, any port in a storm. Forcing myself to think things out took my mind off of my discomfort, and also off of my desperate mind-numbing fear. And disgust. I had thought that Plan C was bad, but it's a walk in the park compared with Plan D.

In the event, Tooth-Bearer moved before Joe and Brother Bear. Khazretgali's raiding party rode back in, hooting and hollering, Khaz at the lead; he had some kind of small sack tied at his saddle that bumped and swayed and leaked blood. I wondered what poor slob he'd killed to slake his evil passions. He glanced my way, and then vanished into his tent with a couple of his men, taking the sack with him.

A minute or so later, his men emerged again and headed in my direction. I gulped, as best as I could with a gag in my mouth and a post-nasal drip. I didn't want to go into that tent. And then several things all happened at once.

First, Tooth-Bearer appeared, and stepped inside Khazretgali's tent. He nodded familiarly at the guards as he passed. He seemed calm, relaxed, at ease, nothing at all like a man about to stage a coup.

At the same time, and from a different direction, several men I recognized from my honor guard of that morning moved to intercept the pair of Khazretgali's men who were coming to get me. They talked and joked with each other as they walked, and had very much the air of just happening to be there.

That was the foreground. The background was rather more dramatic.

I was not able to tell the different clans apart by their dress. But all over the camp, just as Tooth-Bearer entered Khazretgali's tent and the men of my honor-guard blocked Khazretgali's henchmen just two yards in front of me, men turned to those with whom they'd been working or talking or joking a moment before, and with no change of expression drew their knives and set to work. Khaz had been a minor chief, and his clan had been a small one. It had been represented in Corey Park out of proportion to its size—he wasn't a complete fool, and had wanted men about him that he could trust—but there were still few enough that Tooth-Bearer's much larger clan could execute them in one fell swoop.

The slaughter began and ended in moments, and as it ended and the Mingols of other clans began to look up, Tooth-Bearer stepped out of the Great Chief's tent with Great Chief's head, and Tooth-Bearer's men cut the ropes that bound me to the Infernal Tree of Great Bumpiness and removed my gag.

There was no further violence. There wasn't even any great amount of surprise. As my honor guard escorted me to where Tooth-Bearer stood, head in hand, I realized that everyone in camp had been expecting it. Everyone except Khazretgali and his men, who had been blinded by arrogance. When Khaz had taken it upon himself to execute Tooth-Bearer's man out-of-hand, it could have ended no other way, and all of the clans had known it. Possibly, they'd even welcomed it.

Now that the deed was done, there was a moment of watchful waiting.

Would Tooth-Bearer be able to take over? Would the other major chiefs oppose him? And that's where I came in. As I reached Tooth-Bearer I saw three similarly dressed Mingols approaching, each backed by a sizable body of men. I gathered that they were the three other major chiefs; and as they came in three sizes, small, medium, and large, and they each had scraggly little beards, I found myself christening them the Three Billy-Goats Gruff. Their swords and those of their followers were sheathed for the moment; how long would that last?

I turned from them to glare at Tooth-Bearer, though I didn't say anything. Cursing; performing monkeys; you know the drill. But if a shaman's glare held any power, Tooth-Bearer should have withered away where he stood. Instead, he just raised his head.

"I would not have let him kill you," he said quietly, gesturing with that appalling head. He held it by the hair, clamping the absurd hat with the eagle in place with one bony thumb. "I would not have let him kill you, but it was better thus." He waved the head to a spot at his left hand.

I snorted—well, be fair, I'd been snorting for a good bit of the morning, given the state of my sinuses, but I meant it this time—and took the offered spot. Together we faced the approaching Billy-Goats.

Dignity and steely resolve, I thought, and tried to stand as tall and straight as I could. Just a little while more, and Tooth-Bearer and all the other Mingols would be gone for good. Good riddance to them, and a pox on all their houses.

The discussions took a while. There was general agreement that Tooth-Bearer had done a Good Thing; none of the Billy-Goats had relished taking orders from a jumped-up minor chief, and the provocation meant that no other outcome had been possible. But that note of peace and concord sounded for moments only, and then the discord and cacophany began.

I won't try to give a blow-by-blow of the whole set of negotiations. Tooth-Bearer argued that dwelling in our town would weaken the clans, and that all the Mingols should return to their homes and their old ways. The chiefs of a few of the smaller clans agreed with him, not that anyone paid them any attention; the rest, and all three of the Goats, wanted the raids to continue indefinitely, especially so long as there was chocolate and ice cream for the taking. At one point I suggested that they could simply *pay* for these things, and be welcome to them, but they all looked at me blankly for a long moment before resuming their quarrels. After that I kept my mouth shut.

Several hours into it they did find one more point of agreement: our town was a nice place to visit but they wouldn't want to live here full-time. After that the talk turned to the bridge.

Apparently Khaz hadn't mentioned the one-way nature of the bridge until after the chiefs and their men had made the journey to our world-line. That bit of deception hadn't set well, and was one of the reasons that killing him was regarded as a Good Thing. If Tooth-Bearer's new shaman could arrange to make it a two-way trip, that would be a Good Thing, too. And if Tooth-

Bearer wanted to claim the title "chief of chiefs" on the strength of that, well, they'd rather grant the title to him than to a jumped-up little so-and-so like Khaz. At that point the Little Billy-Goat Gruff called for strong drink and they all spent half-an-hour or so ceremonially reviling Khazretgali's name.

I have to hand it to Tooth-Bearer. He had been accepted as the Great Chief on the basis of providing two-way transport between Corey's End and the Steppes of Upper Mingolia—and I suspected that his life wasn't going to be worth much once the Billy-Goats discovered that they'd been fooled. TB might come out of it OK, he might not; but at the very least he was willing to sacrifice his own life for that of the clans. He was a treacherous, vermin-infested stinker, but he was no coward.

Of course, it all came down to whether or not Tooth-Bearer's new shaman really *was* a shaman. It was all very well for Tooth-Bearer to claim that I was a shaman, but the other chiefs wanted to see me do some shamaning. I'm nearly certain that "shamaning" isn't even a word, but that's how my finder translated it. TB acted insulted that they would question his word, but after considerable bickering the Largest Billy-Goat Gruff silenced them all with a roar. He waved at me and said with finality, "If he's a shaman, let him shaman." And they all turned and looked at me.

I did my best to look disdainful, but inside hope was soaring. I had no need to confer with Tooth-Bearer. We were now back on track according to our original plan, and my next steps were clear.

Chapter 17

Tooth-Bearer's men cleared a space around the bridge platform, on which riders were still appearing once a minute or so. The first step was to see if I could do something about that.

As I turned toward the platform, Tooth-Bearer whistled up one of his men, who joined me.

"I am the brother of Sue," he said.

"Hail, Brother-of-Sue," I said. "Your brother was a brave man. Try to make sure no one puts a knife in my back while I'm working, OK? It distracts me."

He snorted. I grimaced. Bravura is easy; bravery is hard.

Ponies have teeth at one end and hooves at the other, so I was careful to approach the bridge platform from the side. I wasn't sure when the next Mingol and his pony were going to show up, and if I startled the beast I didn't want to be the one who paid for it. As I neared, I studied the platform.

The metal traceries adorning the platform had originally formed an arch, now broken off at uneven heights, and not at all by chance the taller of the two uprights was on the side I picked. I was going to have to lay hands on this thing, and I didn't want to have to bend over or kneel down. Dignity—always dignity.

Which reminded me. When I was taken captive, the late unlamented Khaz had had me gagged so that I couldn't do any magic. That wouldn't have stopped me, of course, had I been able to reach one of my finders—no spoken words were necessary. So why had he thought that gagging me would be useful?

Mentally, I gave Red Mustache two points. He'd been an idiot, but he was clever enough to put on a little show so that no one would suspect the true source of his power. That was an excellent idea. A little chanting, a little muttering, a little waving of the arms was most certainly called for. I stretched out my arms to both sides and tried to think of something to chant that would be both impressive and unintelligible to my listeners. Given my finder's translation feature, that was a toughie.

OK, so no loud chanting, then. Perhaps a touch of muttering. In high school I'd been made to memorize Marc Antony's speech from *Julius Caesar*, perhaps I'd use that. But if anyone heard me, that would give the game away. Then it came to me: I needed to use something untranslatable, something for which the Mingols would have no referent. Something like....

Almost under my breath, I began, "Proc howdy open-curly-brace ess close-curly-brace open-curly-brace carriage-return puts double-quote hello new world double quote carriage-return..."

As I muttered I studied the purplish metal of the upright with its glowing blue marks. Then I closed my eyes tightly, remembering how my father's finder had responded when I touched it for the first time, and laid my right palm on the rough, mottled surface.

Even through my closed eyelids the blue pulse was almost blinding, and I heard a roar of surprise and dismay from the assembled Mingols, who were now standing in a wide circle around the platform. I think my two finders pulsed at the same time, though I couldn't be sure.

I'd like to say that I felt some kind of internal response to touching the platform—that I made contact with it in some way, that it responded to me, that I could somehow enter into a dialog with it, and tell it what I wanted, and have it explain to me in some inchoate wordless way just how to do that. That it was glad to have someone to talk to, and that it was eager to help me, like some big, happy, simple-minded dog. The Mingols would vanish, never to be seen again, and I'd head home to Bernie, a much-needed bath, and a bottle of Newcastle Brown.

Unfortunately, that only happens in stories. In my case, there was just a flash and a pulse and a roar from the crowd, and there I was, still wondering what to do.

The platform was clearly related to my finders, and no doubt could be controlled in a similar way...but I had no way to know the details. Best to stick to what I knew. Hah! I almost snorted audibly, but instead I kept muttering source code.

Leaving my right hand on the upright, I held this thought clearly in my mind: I wanted to find the other half of this bridge, this bridge that I was touching, this bridge that had just pulsed blue. I wanted to go there, I wanted to take this half of the bridge with me, I wanted to take Brother-of-Sue with me as well. It was kind of like accessing a value in a complicated data structure: you have to start with something you have, and follow the linkages until you get what you want. I reached out my left hand, palm out, in the same plane as my right hand, so that it was over the open space to the left of the platform, just where I wanted the upright of the upstream platform to be when we arrived. Then I brought my hands together and finished my muttering with a hearty "Exit!"

Then I took a deep breath, and hoping that the upstream platform wasn't pushed up against a wall I reached into the jacket of my Skywalker suit, through the hole in the armpit of my T-shirt, and pressed the button. There was a wordy moment of timeless excess, and everything changed around me.

It worked a treat. One moment the space on my left was empty; the next, it contained a platform and trellis of wrought metal that differed from the one on my right only in that it was somewhat less battered.

I leaned heavily on the uprights for a moment...but only for a moment. A Mingol warrior and his pony were preparing to take the step to Corey Park when we arrived, and the pony—an ill-natured, quarrelsome brute, I've no doubt—and as an aside, isn't

it amazing the way pets come to resemble their owners?—
anyway, the pony objected in the strongest possible terms, rearing
and then backpedaling and pulling on the reins held in its rider's
gloved fist.

The uprights were between me and the pony, so I was perfectly
safe. That's easy for you to say. But it's a surprise to have a
pony go berserk two feet in front of you, so I took a quick step
back, right into Brother-of-Sue. That worthy caught me by the
shoulders and stood me up straight. I'm sure he didn't move an
inch.

After that, I had a moment to look around. My first thought
was, "Wow, look at all the *brown*." That seems to be the first
thing I notice, where ever I go—the color. The ground under my
feet was trampled brown dirt; the sky above was the same color,
though a few shades lighter. It wasn't cloud, or smog, or smoke,
for the sun, a brilliant tan, was plainly visible, and its heat struck
me like a blow. The land was flat to the horizon in all directions,
with just a hint of mountains or hills in the far distance to the
east. There were no trees to be seen, but outside of our
immediate vicinity the trampled brown dirt gave way to dirty
brown grass. I wondered if spring ever came to this desolate
land. Then I thought about the sky, and the sun, and wondered
if maybe this *was* spring. Then I thought that I'd really like to go
somewhere that wasn't flat and monochrome. How come I never
ended up in a place like Hawaii?

I didn't have much time to ponder, though, because more
immediate concerns were crying for my attention. You know,
like the Mingols in all directions, and the officious-looking
Mingol on the opposite side of the bridge platforms who was
scowling at me and wringing his hands like a squirrel. He was
smaller than the average Mingol, and more finely dressed, if
"fine" is the word I'm looking for, and by his manner was clearly
the man in charge. He glanced at the riders lined up in good
order behind the upstream half of the bridge, and then up at the
angle of the sun, and if he'd had a clipboard I'm sure he'd have
frowned at it.

"You there!" he shouted in a high-pitched, whistling voice. "Come here this moment!" Obediently, Brother-of-Sue and I walked around the downstream half of the bridge (since there were no ponies in that direction). "That's Khazretgali's brother," said Brother-of-Sue quietly. "He is in charge of the camp here."

Khazretgali's brother glanced at the sun again, and wrinkled his nose at us. He was tapping his foot on the ground. I half-expected him to pull out his pocket watch and tell me how late he was. He was dirty and grimy and dressed in brown, and if this were Wonderland instead of Upper Mingolia I'd have called him the Brown Rabbit.

I was undismayed by his signs of impatience. I'd already accomplished the most important part of my mission: I'd stopped the influx of Mingols. I didn't think anyone here but me could take the downstream platform back to Corey's End, so that was all right, and my right hand was still in my coat, resting on my finder. If the Brown Rabbit got too annoying I could simply execute Plan A, and be gone.

I'd rather complete my mission than do that, of course, but it felt good to have Plan A as an option again.

The Brown Rabbit looked us up and down. "Who are you," he said, "and what word do you bring me from the Great Khazretgali? Be quick! I have several hundred men here to send to the New Lands before sundown."

Brother-of-Sue stepped forward. "I am Brother-of-Sue, bodyguard to the Great Khazretgali. This is the Great Khazretgali's new Shaman, the Little Climber, kinsman to Red Mustache."

The Rabbit wrinkled his nose at us again, as though he smelled something unpleasant. I suppose he did. *I* did, anyway. He said nothing.

"Chief Kubajin has received permission from the Great Khazretgali for himself and those of his clan to return to the Steppes of Outer Mingolia," Brother-of-Sue lied. "The ends of the bridge must be moved so they can do so. The Great Khazretgali has sent the Little Climber here to arrange for this, and sent me with him to bring you this word."

Kubajin was one of the minor chiefs; I wonder if he had known that Brother-of-Sue was going to take his name in vain.

The Rabbit looked sour. "And why did he send you, rather than one from his own clan?"

"None could be spared. The townsmen are weak, and the hordes have already conquered much land and won great riches. The Great Khazretgali needs his kinsmen to administer his new territories."

"Then why does Kubajin wish to bring his people back to Mingolia?"

Brother-of-Sue smirked. "I said that he had received permission, not that he had requested it. He has angered the Great Khazretgali, who has refused to grant him any share in the new conquests."

The Brown Rabbit warmed up a bit. He still looked disapproving of the whole thing, but I could tell that he liked the idea of Kubajin being taken down a peg. I wondered what he'd do when he found out what was *really* going on. Most likely it would be a short, sharp shock.

"Oh, very well," he said. "Get on with it." Dismissing us, he turned to his aide. "Tell those waiting to cross to make camp."

I was feeling perfectly relaxed when I stepped up to the upstream platform. Getting here was the hard part; it had been reasonable to think that I could use the relation between the upstream and downstream halves of the bridge as an anchor, but until I'd actually done it it had only been a conjecture. Getting home, though, I'd done before. Easy as pie.

I laid my palms on one upright of the upstream half of the bridge, and I thought to myself, "I want to return to Corey Park, in the town of Corey's End, the town in which my mother lives, and I want to take this half of the bridge with me." With this held firmly in my mind, I let go of the bridge and tucked both hands inside my coat. I tried to make it look like some kind of ritual gesture, for the last thing I wanted was for anyone there to realize there was anything important nestled in my armpit.

Then, chanting softly under my breath I pressed down firmly on the button of my finder.

There was a worrying moment of exceeding timefulness, during which absolutely nothing happened. Well, I say nothing. Actually, I could feel all eyes on me, and sweat began to trickle down my face. Ponies stamped, and neighed, and made other horsy noises. The sun beat down. Everything stank, despite which my stomach rumbled, and I thought yearningly of the granola bars taped to my stomach. I'd thought I was so clever, making sure that I couldn't possibly lose them, so I'd have them when I needed them. Now I couldn't get at them without looking a fool in front of the Brown Rabbit. I should have stuck a few in a pocket.

I should have worn a suit with pockets.

I pressed the button again, concentrating on the upstream platform and on my mother. Still nothing happened, and I began to panic. Why wasn't it working? Mom was my anchor, the one person in all of the worlds that I could always return to. I'd been careful to follow all the pointers. It had worked before, when I brought Bernie and me back from the Old City. It had to work. I pressed the button over and over.

The sun beat down. The sweat continued to trickle. The ponies continued to stink.

I pressed the button again.

I dropped my hands to my sides, hanging my head. I had to think. I *hate* having to think in real-time. That's why I always try to find all of the bugs before I deliver the code—so that I don't have to debug with the client hanging over me and reminding me that he's losing thousands of dollars a minute for as long as the website is down. This, needless to say, was much worse.

I forced myself to think. Mom was my anchor. I ought to be able to reach her. Could that flash when I touched the downstream platform have overloaded my finder? No, because if it had I'd still be in Corey Park. And anyway, if my finder was broken I was stuck. Mentally, I tossed that to the side. OK, so Mom was my anchor, but the finder couldn't reach her. Did I have any other anchor? My father, I thought, if he was still alive...but finding him wouldn't get me home. Well, what about Bernie?

Bernie. I thought about Bernie—her blonde hair, her dark eyes. Her laughter. Her anger and indignation when someone she loved got hurt. Her willingness to go the extra mile, at whatever cost. That last bit had nearly gotten me shot, but on the whole I decided to forgive it. Bernie. Mercurial Bernie. Tall, beautiful, blonde-haired Bernie. Take me and the upstream platform to Bernie, I thought. I tucked my hands back in my coat and pressed the button.

The heat and the dirt and the stench and the ponies all vanished. There was an expectant moment of timely relief.

I found myself standing in the parking lot of Dino's Burgers and More, my stomach rumbling loudly enough I expected the drivers going down the street to turn and look. I felt light-headed, and the smell of the cooking burgers took me by the throat and wouldn't let go. I *had* to get something to eat. What a happy coincidence, I thought. Food! Food I liked. Gotta get some food.

Then I remembered my mission, and looked around for the bridge platform. It was beside me, neatly filling the handicapped spot. That might be a problem—I hoped the cops wouldn't give it a ticket, but there wasn't anything I could do about it at the moment. And, oh my! I hoped nobody stood on it. Short of running down the street and buying some hazard tape there wasn't anything I could do about that either, and I wasn't running anywhere until I'd eaten something. I turned back to the restaurant, and through the window I could see a table, and at the table was Bernie, eating a cheeseburger. Bliss!

It had worked: the finder had come through for me. Why I could find Bernie but not my mother I wasn't sure. I hoped Mom was OK. But it was with a palpable sense of relief that I trotted—quickly and somewhat unsteadily—into the restaurant.

Bernie was sitting at a table by herself, not far from the door.

She didn't look up as I came in. I threw myself into the seat across from, almost giddy with relief at being home, and snagged a handful of her french fries. Turn-about is fair play, as they say. They were excellent, as always, golden-brown and delicious, salty and good, and they hit the spot. Comfort food at its simplest.

"There you are," I said, grinning like an idiot around a mouthful of potato. "How come you're here, instead of with Brother Bear?" I shook my head, swallowing. "Never mind that. I've got the bridge platform outside; we need to get a truck or something and some men and get it over to Corey Park. Oh, and do you know if Mom's OK? I couldn't 'find' her. I think something's happened to her."

Bernie looked down at me in surprise, and not in a good way.

"Hey, those aren't yours," she said, her voice sharp and angry. Her dark eyes flashed, and her eyebrows drew together and bristled.

I recoiled. This was *not* the reception I'd expected. She stole my french fries; why shouldn't I steal hers? I opened my mouth to ask that question, but she cut me off.

"I don't know who you are, kid, and I don't know where your mother is, and what makes you think you can help yourself to my lunch?" She looked at me from under her blonde eyebrows like I was some loathsome new species of insect and she wanted to squash me, the needs of scientific investigation be damned.

I stared at her, the french fries turning to lead in my gut. Have you ever been hungry and queasy at the same time? I don't recommend it. I got slowly out of my seat and backed away, still staring. I looked around the restaurant, Dino's Burgers and More, as it ever was.

But Dino's had burned to the ground.

This wasn't Dino's. Not *my* Dino's. This wasn't my Bernie. This Bernie didn't know me. This Bernie's eyebrows were blonde.

I was in the wrong place. This wasn't my world-line. In this world-line Bonnie Tyler never met a tall, dark stranger in philosophy class, married him, and moved to Corey's End. In this world, Michael Henderson was never born, never grew up, was never small for his age. This Bernie had never met him, never pointed a gun at him, never—dared I think it?—fallen in love with him.

This Was Not My Home.

I must have looked pretty bad, because the outrage in Not-Bernie's eyes began to be replaced by concern. It was too much. It was just what I would have expected. She wasn't my Bernie, but she acted like my Bernie.

"Hey, kid, are you OK?" she said.

I shook my head, still staring, still backing away. She started to rise, and my nerve broke. Turning from her I stumbled out of the restaurant, out of Not-Dino's, to where the bridge platform waited. I felt like I was running in slow motion, like one of those nightmares where the nameless monster is just behind you and you can hardly run and when you get to your house you stagger inside and slam the door and it won't latch no matter how many times you try, except that in those dreams the monster waits patiently for you to get the door locked, but in this one Not-Bernie was still following me. But I made it to the platform, and hanging onto the left-hand upright with one hand, I grabbed at my finder with the other and pressed the button. As I pressed it I looked back; Not-Bernie was just coming out the door.

There was a horrible moment of anguished anticipation, and then I was falling.

Chapter 18

Did you notice that I pushed the button without thinking about where I was going?

One of the few advantages of being small for your age is that if you trip, you don't have as far to fall, and you're not as likely to be seriously hurt. But it isn't a sure thing, and while it's a help in certain situations, it's still a good idea to look before you leap. And when you're using a finder, and can't see where you're going to end up, it's even more important to look before you leap (if that makes sense).

Please note, I'm not saying this just to heighten the tension. It's something I really, really, really want to remember.

Anyway, the next thing I knew I was falling through the air, still clinging to the bridge platform with one hand, spray wetting my face and a roaring sound in my ears. I had a confused impression of sky and gray stone and black gaping windows and tumbling water as I grabbed onto the upright with my other hand and both legs and clung there for dear life. It hurt—the jagged surface of the upright was going to leave marks on my arms and legs—but I wouldn't have let go for any amount of money.

Grabbing on like that may have been a mistake. Pulled by my weight, insignificant as it might be, the platform turned in the air and the wind of our passage caught at its base and flipped it upside-side down and my stomach rebelled.

If being queasy and ravenous at the same time is bad, vomiting up a handful of french fries while screaming in terror and riding a trans-dimensional bridge head-first into an abyss of gray stone and falling water is worse. And I was still ravenous. And wet. And cold.

The spray got into my eyes, and I had to blink like mad to clear them. Through wet lashes I saw a long thin tracery of twisted purple metal go by to my left, seemingly close enough to touch. I was glad I hadn't hit it, and wondered how long I my luck would hold out.

Luck. Hah!

In a frozen moment I knew where I was. I had seen it before, though not from this point of view. I was in the Old City, falling down the chasm in the deserted square. The wind whistled in my ears, and the roar of the falling water was nearly deafening, and I began to shiver.

Even from this privileged vantage point I couldn't see the bottom of the chasm: it seemed to go on forever until it was lost in mist and darkness. I wondered if I would see the bottom before I made its acquaintance.

Then over the noise of wind and water, not to mention my own screaming, I heard the harsh thrumming that heralded the Giant Hairy Mutant Locusts of Doom. If I hadn't been too caught up in the moment to think, I'd have rolled my eyes and heaved a sigh. Mutant Locusts of Doom were all I needed.

Another branch of purple metal appeared below me in the mist. This one really was close enough to touch: it caught one corner of the bridge platform with an enormous clang and sent the platform tumbling. I was nearly torn loose but somehow I held on. I saw a little square of sky far above, and then the mist below, and then the sky, and then the mist, and then I lost the rest of my french fries.

By now you're probably jumping up and down and shrieking, "Your finder! Push the button on your finder, you idiot! *Get out of there!*" Well, yes, that would be the logical thing to do. All I can say is, if you think it's easy to think logically while cold, wet, hungry, and queasy, tumbling down into a bottomless chasm, surrounded by water and flying buttresses of wrought metal, striking any one of which square on would be enough to permanently vitiate my future career (unless of course I hit bottom first, which would have the same effect) with the strong possibility of being devoured, alive or dead, by the Metal-Winged Locusts of Doom, *and* without having rid my hometown of a horde of murderous, stinking, blood-thirsty barbarians, well, then, if you think that's easy, *you* try it.

And anyway, it isn't like I was taking my time, reading the paper and enjoying the scenery. Things happen quickly when you're falling, whether you're small for your age or not. And I couldn't just push the button—I might end up somewhere worse. And I had to finish throwing up first.

After I was done with that, and long before I was bored, it was time to take steps. This was definitely a Plan A situation. "Somewhere safe," I thought, convulsively, over and over, "somewhere safe. Take me to somewhere safe." My right hand was clamped onto the metal work so hard that my knuckles were white, and it didn't want to let go, but somehow I managed to detach it and wiggle it into my coat.

The thrumming noise had been getting steadily louder. As I got my hand onto my finder the platform happened to be turned so that I was looking downwards, and I saw a dark movement in the mist below me. Movement as of something, of many things, rising up toward me much faster than my velocity could account for. It looked like—I won't say what it looked like. I don't want to know what it looked like.

I pushed the button.

There was a desperate moment of screaming and pain, and then there was a loud *THUNK* as the top of the bridge platform's arch buried itself in red dust and gravel several feet above my head—or, rather, below my head, because I was still upside-down. And then, because the arch extended from one end of the base of the platform, making an L-shape, it over-balanced and tipped over with another loud thunk, making a sort of lean-to of purple metal. I let go of the upright and fell to the ground, gasping for breath and shivering despite the burning heat.

I don't know how long I lay there, but eventually my heartbeat slowed enough for my hunger to reassert itself. Without rising I rolled onto my back, pulled open my coat, and tore at the tape holding the granola bars to my stomach. My left arm wasn't happy, but I ignored that. First things first. My trembling fingers had no luck opening the wrapper of the first bar, and I tore at it with my teeth. The bar was crushed and broken when I got it open, but I didn't care. I poured it into my mouth. Bliss. I ate another, and another, and another, and another, and then I found my water bottle and drank a long drink of water. And then fatigue came down on me like a hammer, and I passed out right there in the dust, heedless of the rocks digging into my back.

I woke up some unknown time later, still hungry but not ravenous. I hurt all over, and I could hardly move my left arm for the stabbing pain in my shoulder. I must have wrenched it when the platform had hit the flying buttress and sent it tumbling. I rolled carefully onto my right side, and got my right hand under me. Then, little by little I worked my way up into a sitting position. That might be easier for me than for you under the same circumstances, but it was still one of the harder things I'd ever done. My right arm was usable, unlike my left, but I can't truthfully say that it was what you'd call happy to be of service.

Once more or less vertical I looked around as best I could without moving too much. I couldn't see behind me; turning was painful, and anyway the base of the platform was in the way. But in front of me, and to the sides, was an all-too-familiar expanse of red desert. And in the near distance was a crumpled mass of wood and canvas that I was confident had been a tent until a few days prior.

I was just outside Red Mustache's bolt hole. I knew it had to be the same world line I'd been to before, or the ruined tent wouldn't be there. The Red Desert might exist in any number of world-lines, but that tent had been put there by a Traveler, and there was no reason for it to be there otherwise.

I didn't know whether to laugh or cry. I could get to the Old City without any trouble, and to the Red Desert, but I couldn't get *home*. And then I knew perfectly well whether to laugh or cry, and I did.

Then I had some more granola bars, and a swallow of water, and then I got to my feet and went to look over the remains of the tent as best I could with one working arm.

It look a while, but the results were encouraging. Apparently the big galumphing beast that had chased Bernie and me had knocked it down and maybe stepped on it, but neither it nor its giant master had indulged in any further destruction. The wooden supports had snapped, so even if I'd been in good shape I wouldn't have been able to set it all up again the way it had been but I was able to salvage the cot, the rations, and the water. I can't say that I liked pepper crackers and merchant oil, but at least I wouldn't starve—or die of thirst—while I figured out what to do.

Judging that the lean-to formed by the upside-down bridge platform was better shelter than anything I was likely to manage to build from the remains of the tent, I dragged my loot there a little a time. The cot was the hardest thing to move, being big and bulky; it was made to come apart, but I wasn't sure I'd be able to assemble it again one-handed. After a long time, with many rests, I managed to drag it over the dust and gravel, and once it was positioned carefully in the shade of the platform I settled down on it to think.

When I woke up it was dark but for the light of a million stars. I looked at them for a while, not thinking. Despair caught at my heart, and the stars were no consolation. Then I had a drink of water, and wrapped myself up in the blanket again. Maybe things would look better in the morning.

I spent most of the next day lying on the cot in the shade of the bridge platform, thinking. It was too hot to go anywhere, and there was nowhere to go: just endless red dirt and rocks, crowned in the middle distance by shimmering waves of heat. The air was still, and too hot, and dry with it. I was glad Red Mustache had left plenty of water. Every so often I drank a toast to him as I took a swig.

Mostly I thought about how few things there were in the world —in all the worlds—that I could truly call my own. Me, for example. I was my own. Like the commercial says, I never left home without me. I was ubiquitous: wherever I went, why, there I was! There was no getting rid of me. Like the cat, I kept coming back. Like a bad penny, I kept turning up. But what a value for a penny! Penny for penny, Pound for pound, I'd stack me up against any Viking or Mingol you'd care to name. Compact, that's what I was. Concentrated. A pint-sized powerhouse. Easy to pack, and easy to store between trips. I didn't make messes in the house, and I didn't cost much to feed because I didn't eat much.

Well, except when Traveling. But I gather that most people make pigs of themselves when they're away from home. Travel, they say, is broadening.

Looking back on it, it's just possible that I was a tad delirious. My left shoulder was still on fire, and it hurt to move. But mostly I thought such silly things to keep my mind off of the two other things I could truly call my own: my parents.

My mom was my own, my very own, my own mother. There was no one else in the whole world—in all the worlds—of whom I could say, "Her! She's my mom." That's what made her an anchor. And I didn't want to think about her, because I was nearly certain she was dead.

Everything she had told me, and all of my (admittedly limited) experience, were clear that my mother was an anchor for me, someone my finder should always be able to locate. You *can* go home again...as long as you remember that home is people, not a place. And yet, when I tried to "find" her, nothing happened. I'd tried repeatedly in Mingolia; and I'd tried a number of times when I woke up that morning. I didn't budge. Mom didn't seem to be there to be found.

I tried not to think of Khazretgali's evil grin, or the bloody, dripping bag he'd carried into his tent moments before Tooth-Bearer had taken his life. If that bag contained what I thought it did, well, I was already avenged. Tooth-Bearer had seen to that.

Revenge isn't sweet; I don't care what they say.

Well, and then there was my father. I still couldn't bring myself to call him my "dad". Was he alive or dead? I didn't know. Mom thought he must be dead; if he were alive, he'd have returned to her. She was certain of it. Me, I write software. To write software that works, you need to think of all the things that could possibly go wrong, and make sure they won't, or handle them if they do. It's good practice for brooding.

So I could think of several ways my father might be alive somewhere out there in the worlds. When he'd left us he'd been on the run, so he said, desperate to lead his enemies away from his wife and child. Perhaps he got caught, and killed, or Traveled to somewhere deadly in the heat of the chase. That's what Mom thought. Or perhaps they caught him and took away the finder he'd stolen. Then they might have kept him prisoner, or more likely simply dumped him somewhere. With no finder, he could never return...and it was unlikely he'd run across another one.

Or maybe, just maybe, he was a lying treacherous bastard. He'd needed a son to carry on his line; he'd provided that son with a finder; and then he'd gone on about his life, with never a second thought.

Mom didn't think so. But then, she wouldn't.

According to her, my father had spent his life studying what it meant to be a Traveler, and how it all worked. If I could "find" him, and if I didn't get killed or imprisoned myself, maybe he'd have some ideas as to how I could get home.

I put that idea to the side for the moment. Whatever my mom said, I thought there was a good probability that he was a lying treacherous bastard, and no one to go looking for. And in any event, I was in no shape to go on another wild journey through the world-lines. I wouldn't move from where I was until I had my ducks in a row or the food and water ran out. Of course, once the water ran out I'd have no place to put the ducks, which would be a pity—they'd look so cute, all bright and yellow, lined up next to each other. I wondered how many of them I had? One, two, three.... I shifted on the cot, and winced at the stabbing pain in my shoulder.

Have I mentioned that I might have been delirious?

Anyway, Mom and I were my father's anchors in Corey's End. If I couldn't get back there, neither could he.

And that was it. I had no siblings, and no children. My grandparents—my mother's parents—had both died before I was born. My father's parents—well, I suppose he must have had some, but who knows where they were, or whether they were still alive. If I wasn't going to go looking for him, I certainly wasn't going to go looking for them.

Bernie, my beloved Bernie, she wasn't mine at all. I'd verified that empirically.

What was the phrase Mom had used? "Ontologically significant." For someone to be an anchor for me, the relationship had to be "ontologically significant." I was hazy on the specifics, but I gathered it meant that the relationship had to be part of my very being. Knowing Bernie didn't make me a different person...but my mother and father had made me a person to begin with. It's a different order of relationship altogether.

Mom had also said that marriage was ontologically significant "if you do it right." I wondered what that meant. I was willing to take it on faith, though, and I resolved to do something about it as soon as ever I got the chance.

At the moment it didn't seem likely.

Chapter 19

The day wore on. The shadow of the bridge platform moved across the red dust. I watched it pass one little rock after another, and every so often I got up and dragged the cot to match, cursing at the pain in my useless shoulder. I stared at the horizon. Once in a while I nibbled crackers and sipped water.

Around the middle of the afternoon an intermittent breeze came up, raising small clouds of red dust that stuck to my hot, sweaty body and made me cough and choke. I took off the coat of my Skywalker suit and put it over my head to block the dust, and when I was done my shoulder felt much, much worse. Then I remembered the blanket and cursed a little more. I could have put the blanket over my head, and left the coat on.

I lay there with the coat over my face for a long while, thinking of nothing much and trying not to move. I hurt. I had nowhere to go, except everywhere I didn't want to be. I knew of no way to get home. Thinking was useless. And I hurt! So I just lay there, my heart and my stomach both clenched, weeping dry tears.

After a time of frozen despair I began to slip into that half-dreaming, half-waking state you get when you're sick in bed on a hot afternoon. My thoughts began to wander this way and that through my life, and in time I began to daydream about my father and what his life with Mom might have been like, in those days just before and after I was born.

It had been a life of ease, I knew that. He must have had plenty of money before he ever met Mom, because she'd never had to work while I was growing up, and I don't remember ever having had any sense that we had to scrimp and save. He must have left her quite a pile.

He hadn't worked, either...at least, not for a paycheck, not in Corey's End. He'd gone to college as a grown man because there was something he'd wanted to learn; and while there he'd met one Bonnie Tyler, and married her, and they'd moved to Corey's End, a town where they knew nobody, where he could continue with his studies in peace.

As I imagined their life together, I thought that he hadn't been social, that he seldom even left the house—at least, not by the front door. From Mom I knew that he'd Traveled all over the place, but he didn't need to leave the house to do that. Corey's End was his home base, his safe-house, his place of safety. He didn't want to be known there, because to be known is to be a target. Both Plan A and Plan B are so much easier if no one knows you, if no one sees you, if no one even knows you're around, if no one is acquainted with you. If no one knows you, no one envies you, no one hates you, no one wants to do you dirty.

My father wanted to slip through the worlds, unheard, unseen, avoiding notice, avoiding trouble, pursuing his dream of understanding the finders, and working out the rules and principles by which Traveling worked. He didn't need to attract attention to do that. He'd gotten a fortune somehow, to support his work, and I supposed that he must have attracted some attention in gaining it. Perhaps there were world-lines where enterprises he'd started were still going concerns; perhaps some of his Travels had been to those world-lines, to collect the proceeds and bring them back to Corey's End. I wondered how he'd done it. It had seemed to Bernie and I that transporting wealth from one world-line to another without being noticed was a hard thing to do, but clearly he'd managed it.

But he hadn't sought or wanted the attention for its own sake, and as soon as he could he'd outrun it, outrun it all the way to another world-line, to Corey's End, where he saw only his wife, and eventually me. I began to feel sorry for him—he must have been a lonely man.

Or perhaps it didn't bother him. Being alone didn't bother me, or at least it hadn't used to. I'd been content with a steady round of work, interacting only with my customers on-line, and leavened by books and computer games. My only human contacts had been with the cashiers at the grocery stores and the various places I had lunch, and at my weekly dinner with Mom. I hadn't skulked at home, though, the way I thought my father had. Ever since I'd left school and moved into the apartment over the garage, Mom had encouraged me to get out on my bike, to go out to lunch, to explore Corey's End. I'd agreed because a knowledge of the local geography is useful for both Plans A and B, and because I got tired of eating cold cereal from the minimart two blocks down. The exercise also kept my weight down. To be small and dressed in primary colors and looking like a ten-year-old is bad enough when you're a twenty-something professional. To be all of those things and also round is to be a beach ball. No thank you.

My father and mother were so different. Mom didn't have to work, but she didn't sit at home watching soap operas and nibbling chocolates. She was involved all kinds of charitable work, she played bridge, she knew all of the storekeepers by name. She was always busy, her phone was always ringing, and it sometimes seemed like she knew everyone in town. And they all knew her. How many people had I talked to since the Vikings had first appeared at Dino's who had identified me as "Bonnie Henderson's son"?

Suddenly I was wide awake, lying on the cot, my head shrouded in the stuffy confines of my dusty red coat. Could it be that simple? My heart was racing, and I could feel the first stirrings of hope in my heart. Ruthlessly I suppressed them. I had to think. I had to work it out. I had to make sure. But I could almost see those ducks gathering on the dusty red ground, quacking at each other, waiting for the order to fall into place. I held my breath, feeling that a careless move, a sudden jumping to conclusions, would scatter them to the four winds.

Could it be that simple? I thought of objections. If it was that simple, surely my father would have known it?

Maybe not. He was solitary by nature, and he thought of other people as potential problems, as obstacles, as threats to be worked around or avoided. Perhaps it wouldn't have occurred to him on his own.

But he might have learned it from someone else. But who would he have learned it from? From his father? Not if his father was like him, or if his father had died when he was young. And I gathered that Travelers didn't generally seek out each others' company. Every Traveler would want to pass finders on to his children, and the only way to get more was to take them from other Travelers. If you didn't want to be known by people who couldn't follow you from world-line to world-line, you certainly wouldn't want to be known by people who *could*.

I sat up, pulling my rumpled coat off of my head into my lap, and laughed. Then I gasped at the pain in my shoulder, but first I laughed. If I was right, if I was right! It was too funny. My father had made me small, so that I'd have to learn to run away, to avoid other people. He had made me small, and that had made me sour. My father had given me lemons. But my Mom, God bless her, my Mom had seen how to turn those lemons into lemonade.

I squinted at the late afternoon sunshine. It was hard to see, but it didn't matter, because I wasn't looking at the scenery. Instead, I was watching the little ducks waddling into a ragged line, quacking boisterously, triumph shining from their little ducky faces.

Everyone in town knew my Mom. And everyone in town had seen little Mikey Henderson riding around town on his bike, eating lunch, buying groceries, avoiding eye contact. I didn't know them, *but they knew me!*

And there was only one of me. According to my father,

Travelers were true singulars. In all of infinite number of world-lines, there was only one world where Bonnie Tyler had married my father, only one town where Michael Henderson was born and got older and didn't grow up as much as he would have liked. There was only one town that knew me.

Corey's End might not be *my* town, not in any "ontologically significant" sense. There were infinitely many other Corey's Ends across the world-lines; I'd just been to one of them. But relationships run both ways. Joe McGillicuddy wasn't "mine"; but only one Joe McGillicuddy knew me. Bernie wasn't "mine," as I'd discovered to my shock and horror, but only one Bernie Balducci knew me.

Perhaps she wasn't *my* Bernie—though I intended to fix that—but I was certainly *her* Michael. There was no other Bernie of whom that was true.

A thought struck me. How was it that I'd come to this same place, this Red Desert, twice? I had no ontologically significant anchor here. This Red Desert must exist in a multitude of world lines. The first time I'd come, I'd used Red Mustache's finder, which had some kind of affinity for this particular place, but the second time I'd used my father's. How had I come to the same place?

I'd come here because of the supplies Red Mustache had left here. This was the only world in which this desert had pepper crackers and merchant oil from Calahosis Camping Supply. The merchant oil had no ontologically significant relation with me, not in itself...but its presence here, in this place, was a singular thing, a unique thing.

The quacking fell silent. The ducks were locked into place, all standing at attention in one long row. Some were looking in the direction I most wanted to Travel; the rest were looking at me expectantly. I was right. I knew I was right, and the joy of it filled my heart despite the pain in my shoulder.

What did I want? I wanted to be in Corey Park, with the bridge platform. I wanted to be in Corey Park in the Corey's End that knew me, the Corey's End where Bernie and Joe

McGillicuddy and Brother Bear and Gaius Valens and even Maynard the Recruiting Poster were waiting for me to come back.

When you're small for your age, it's important to have friends.

Moving as quickly as I could, I tucked the cot and blanket and the remaining supplies under the ruins of the tent, to preserve them for next time. I could come back here any time I wanted, and I might well need to some day. My father was a sad, lonely, friendless man, and he had given me lemons, but Plan A was still sometimes the right thing to do.

The sun was setting when I'd finished tidying up. The breeze had died down, and the air was hot and clear and crystalline. I stood next to the half-upside-down bridge platform, looking into the distance and into the heart of Corey's End, my Corey's End, the Corey's End that knew me and maybe even loved me.

I pushed the button.

Chapter 20

That's all there was to it, really. The platform and I appeared back in Corey Park; the Mingols, terrified by my fearsome and disheveled demeanor, hastened *en masse* back over the bridge to Mingolia; the folk of Corey's End, grateful for my self-sacrifice, voted me man of the year; and Bernie married me in a beautiful ceremony attended by everyone in town, up to and including the Mayor of Corey's End and the President of the United States, who had dropped by to get one of Dino's cheeseburgers and was miffed when it wasn't forthcoming.

In fact...well, actually, it was a little more complicated than that. And rather different, too. I totally made up that bit about the President, for example. I suppose I'd better tell it the way it happened.

When I appeared back in Corey Park, Tooth-Bearer was standing just where I'd left him. I was disheveled, in pain, covered with red mud, and in need of a bath. He was short, smelly, and also in need of a bath. He, at least, hadn't changed a bit.

I drew myself up to my full height, such as that was, and looked him in the eye. My shoulder hurt like blazes.

"My mother is dead," I said. My voice sounded strange in my ears, flat, emotionless.

Tooth-Bearer's expression didn't change.

"Khazretgali is dead," he said.

"Many good people are dead," I said.

"And so is Khazretgali," he said, as if he bore no personal responsibility for the carnage of the of the last week. Hate burned in the pit of my stomach, and for moment I wished that I'd left the downstream end of the bridge platform somewhere other than Mingolia—the Old City, say. Then I remembered what I had almost not seen in those last moments in the abyss, and felt ashamed of myself.

Instead, I jerked my head in the direction of the platform, which was still in the lean-to position. "It's time for you to go," I said. "There will be no more deaths. Remember that I can find you where ever you are, any time of the day or night." I wasn't at all sure that that was true, but I salved my conscience by reflecting that I wasn't at all sure that it wasn't.

Tooth-Bearer inclined his head slightly, acknowledging both the threat and my ability to carry it out. I was fortunate that he truly wished to return home. At such a threat Khazretgali would have barked orders, watched my life bubble out onto the ground at his feet, rubbed his hands with glee, and retired to plot further death and destruction for his enemies. Tooth-Bearer simply glanced at several of his men, and then at the platform. In moments it was right side up and the first cohort to return home were lined up with their ponies. Tooth-Bearer had no need to bark, but his bite, as I had seen the day before, was formidable.

No doubt he *was* plotting death and destruction, but the first sign his enemies would see of it would be the knife across their throats...um, so to speak.

I stood and watched the first dozen or so Mingols pass back across the bridge to the Steppes of Upper Mingolia. They all bore the signs of Tooth-Bearer's clan, and were led by his favored lieutenant. They were also armed to the teeth, not that that was unusual for Mingols. After them, one of the lesser chiefs and his clansmen led their ponies up to the platform. I turned my back on them and left. It had taken days for all of the Mingols in Corey's End to arrive; it would take days for them all to return home. I wasn't going to stand and watch the whole thing.

Tooth-Bearer said nothing as I walked away through the assembled Mingol hordes. But four of his men followed behind me on their ponies and escorted me safely out of the park and followed me all the way back to Mary Claire's apartment building. I paid no attention to them, didn't look back to see if they were following, but I knew they were there. While I was still in the park, I wouldn't look back; I was making an exit. When you're small for your age you learn the importance of the theatrical gesture. Once I was out in the street I couldn't look back, because I didn't want my escort to see the tears leaving trails on my dirty red face.

My Mingol honor guard stopped and sat their ponies about twenty feet from the gate of Mary Claire's building. Watchful Romans opened the gate of the parking garage, and I passed within while they stood ready to avenge any final treachery. Whether their vigilance was necessary, I don't know—I don't think it was—but the four Mingols left without incident.

Bernie burst out of the elevator just as the parking garage gate rattled to a close, and came running.

I guess I was standing funny because she said "You're hurt!" Then she got close enough to see me clearly in the dimness of the garage, and recoiled. "Michael, what happened to you? You're filthy!"

"My mother is dead," I said, in the same voice I had used with Tooth-Bearer.

She stared at me just long enough to take in the expression on my face; and then she took me in her arms, and I could let other people worry about things for a while.

Everybody came to the funeral.

Well, I say "everybody". The President of the United States wasn't there. Neither was Mr. Lee of the #1 Fine Grocery. A number of people who'd been injured by the Mingols and were still in the hospital weren't there. Far too many people who'd been killed by the Mingols weren't there, and their mourners weren't there either. My mother's was not the only funeral held that day.

Most especially, the Mingols themselves weren't there, not that they would have been welcome. The last of Tooth-Bearer's men had crossed over the day before, and barring a stray Mingol or two out roaming the countryside they were all gone. The bridge platform stood shrouded in caution tape amidst the sad remains of Corey Park, guarded by a pair of Maynard's colleagues. The clean-up of the park hadn't yet begun, though that would come soon.

(As an aside, the National Guard finally showed up the middle of the next week. By that time it was all over, and nobody would give them the time of day, or even admit that there was anything wrong. We're self-reliant here in Corey's End, and anyway, if they'd wanted to be of help, they'd left it a little late.)

So it wasn't really everybody, but it was still a surprising lot of people. My mother had been well-known and much loved. I didn't recognize most of them, but I knew more of them than I would have expected just a few weeks earlier. Joe was there, and Brother Bear, and Gaius Valens. Gaius' soldiers, rested and spruced up, formed an honor guard. They lined both sides of the center aisle and saluted, right fist on left breast, as the coffin was wheeled to the front of the church.

Bernie and her mother had made the arrangements for the funeral. I'd been in no shape, physically or emotionally, and anyway I wasn't at all sure I wanted a big to-do. Bernie had insisted that a public funeral was needful, and looking at the sea of faces I had to agree that she'd been right.

Bernie and her family had been a solid rock for me ever since I returned home. She'd gotten me to the Emergency Room to get my shoulder looked at, and when I explained about my mother she'd had the good sense to ask Maynard to have police sent to my mother's house to take care of things. She'd also made arrangements with the mortuary and with a cleaning service. I was never told precisely how Mom had died, or just what Khazretgali's men had done. I preferred not to know. I spent the week recovering in the spare room at Bernie's mom's house, and when I finally went home there was only the smell of new paint and new carpeting—and some missing furniture—to show that anything had happened. My room over the garage hadn't even been touched.

During the week when the Mingols were returning home I sometimes woke in the night, shivering with tears and fury. As I lay there, I would think again about Traveling to Mingolia and taking the other end of the bridge to the Old City. The Giant Locusts could have a field day: fresh Mingol for breakfast. And then I'd remember my fall down into the chasm, and that awful thrumming, and what I'd not quite seen rising through the mist, and I'd hate myself.

In the end, I let them go in peace.

I don't remember much of the service, as I was in a bit of a fog. The foot, it would no longer tap. The arms, they would no longer cross. There would be no more Sunday dinner with Mrs. Henderson. I got up when Bernie nudged me and said a few words about my Mom and how grateful I was to her, and I managed to hold it together until I sat down. I think a number of others got up and said things too. But Bernie sat next to me and held my hand, and so that was all right.

When it was over, Gaius Valens' men banged their swords on their shields and carried Mom's coffin out of the church to the waiting hearse. There was a short graveside service, and then it was all over.

Chapter 21

Well, except for the clean-up, both physical and emotional.

When Chief Roderick was quite sure that all of the Mingols had been rounded up and escorted off the property, so to speak, the whole town pitched in to fix the mess that had once been Corey Park. Bernie and I did our part by removing the bridge platform, still festooned with caution tape, and dropping it off in the Red Desert. I was tempted to put it in my backyard and use it for a trellis, but I didn't know how to turn it off, and I couldn't take the risk that some poor soul would stand on it and get the shock of his life.

Several months later I Traveled to Upper Mingolia and retrieved the other half of the bridge. I'd have gone earlier, but I didn't trust Tooth-Bearer or his people not to try to snatch me. Sure, Tooth-Bearer *said* that the high-life in Corey's End was corrupting his people, and that he wanted them to return to their old ways on the Steppes of Upper Mingolia, and maybe he really meant it...but maybe he'd change his mind when the chocolate was all gone. And then, a chief with a court wizard might have more power than a chief without, and I've read that barbarian tribes would sometimes cripple individuals of some essential skill so that they couldn't run off. I'd tried to make sure that none of the Mingols knew about my finder, but why risk it?

So I waited until I thought they'd no longer expect me, and I went by dead of night, and there were no complications. Seriously, no complications at all—I could have gone in broad daylight. The Mingols had moved on and the platform stood in glorious loneliness, covered in brown dust, and haunted only by the stench of their passing. I thought about leaving something for Tooth-Bearer, should he return that way, but my better self prevailed.

It took fifteen minutes' effort, no more, and the downstream platform had joined its better half in the Red Desert. I even swathed it with caution tape I'd brought for the purpose. Then I met Bernie for an early but much-needed breakfast at the Pancake Hut. I tell you truly, after three consecutive jumps there's no such thing as too many carbs. It's the Traveller's Diet —three jumps first thing in the morning, and all the pancakes you can eat. And bacon. Lots of bacon.

Chief Roderick called me down to the Wilson Street Station a few days before the Vikings were to stand trial for looting, breaking and entering, and the killings of an even dozen of my fellow citizens. Jim Lambert, Corey's Ends' district attorney, was with him.

We shook hands, and Lambert got right to the point.

"Mr Henderson," he said, "I've got a problem, and Chief Roderick says he thinks you can help me with it."

"The Vikings?" I asked after a few moments of thought. It took me at least two of those moments just to remember the Vikings, as they'd been completely off my radar for some days.

"That's right," he said. "We know they're guilty. Hell, they've admitted it. If this goes to trial the jury won't even have to leave the room." He hesitated.

"And...." I said, making that get-on-with-it motion with my right hand. Then my heart jerked, remembering my Mom, but I think I managed not to show it.

Lambert grimaced. "I don't know what we'll do with them, Mr. Henderson. They'd have to go to prison...but they are undocumented aliens. Where are they supposed to be from? What am I going to do if some officious busy-body decides we have to deport them? I *really* don't want to have to explain this to anybody at the state or federal level."

I scowled. "You want me to get rid of them for you."

He nodded, and looked apprehensive. "That's right."

I shook my head. "I don't do executions, Mr. Lambert."

He shook his head, saying, "No, no, of course not." I don't *think* he looked disappointed, but it's hard to say; he was a lawyer, after all. "No, we don't do capital punishment in this state, Mr. Henderson. But we'd like them to go *away*, at the very least...and if I could tell the families that justice was done, that would be good too."

So I did that thing. I couldn't take them back to their home world-line, so I found a place that was somewhat similar, and dumped them. They weren't pleased to go, but they didn't make a fuss, either, maybe because I let them take their new clothes with them. Even Charlie Johansen was glad to see them go. Real Vikings, it turned out, were not nearly as pleasant as imagined Vikings. He'd tried having them work in his store, and he'd had complaints about their behavior from both his patrons and his sales staff. I wasn't surprised, remembering the circumstances under which I'd first met them, and after I'd dropped them off I was glad to think that I'd never see them again. For his part, I think Charlie's thinking about becoming a Civil War buff.

"That Red Mustache," Blond Braid said to me as he looked around his new home, "he made lots of promises. He gave us foolish helmets and axes, and he promised us unending wealth and everlasting fame, and a glorious death in battle. Instead, we got this." He looked at me. "If you see Red Mustache again," he said, sternly, "please be killing him for me."

I just said, "Oh, I think you'll be seeing him before I do," which made him happy. I suppressed a shudder, and then I wished them a nice day and left.

The Romans were another story. I offered to try to take them home, feeling that it was the least I could do, but Gaius Valens turned me down flat.

"When the mustached wizard stole us away, we were awaiting battle," he said. In Latin, I *think*. He'd been studying, and heaven help me I couldn't tell the difference. "If you succeed in returning us to our home, I will be executed for desertion and my century will be decimated. There will be lasting disgrace for our families. If you leave us somewhere else like our home, then from what you tell me there will be two of each of us, and that would lead to endless confusion."

I thought of sitting across the table from Not-Bernie at the Not-Dino's, and shuddered. Endless confusion was a wholly inadequate term.

"So should we go somewhere else that is not like our home? No. We will stay here, and Brother Bear will teach me how to drive and how to restore old cars like Joe's Corvette."

This was not as unworkable a scheme as you might think. The tale of the Seige of the Pancake Hut had spread all over town, and the Romans were widely regarded as heroes. They were also young, muscular, and mostly good-looking, except for their teeth, and to a man they were skilled at picking up the language spoken by the local girls. The girls, for their part, were not uninterested. I expected the dentists and orthodontists in town to make a killing over the next several years.

I was concerned that it would take a long time for them all to find jobs, but I needn't have worried. In the immediate aftermath of the Mingol invasion there was lots of physical work to do, and they dove right in. As time went on and they made a little money and got to know us better, a variety of other opportunities were offered to them. Some of them took up gardening and yard work, a task not entirely different from the old soldier's dream of buying a farm when he retires, and if the gardens they maintained looked rather squared off and precise, they were also scrupulously tidy. Several others learned to tend bar, and one of them, Valen's second-in-command, even opened his own business: a physical fitness and weight loss outfit called the Extreme Roman Legion Bootcamp. I see it regularly on my way to Dino's (which was rebuilt with great dispatch and much

Roman labor). The Bootcamp is both popular and effective —"and so authentic!" the ladies tell me, though Gaius assures me that it's anything but.

As for me, well, I'll admit I've still got a lot of unanswered questions. What happened to my father? Will I figure out how to make a living with my finder, or will I keep doing my same old job? And what about Bernie and me? Will she marry me? Will I keep knocking her down? And if she *does* agree to marry me, will it be before or after she kills me? Time will tell. But when you're small for your age, it's good to have things to look forward to.